SARAH M. ANDERSON WRITING AS

MAGGIE CHASE

HIS
CROWN
JEWEL

Acknowledgements

I could not have written this book without the generous help of the following people: Melissa Jolly for everything she does, Tasha Harrison and Mary Dieterich for editing, and Leah Hanlin for designing the book.

Dedication

To my husband, who's all kinds of inspiring.

Chapter One

M istress? You better come."
Emily Weatherspoon looked up from behind her desk to see Samuel Horner poking his head through her office door. "It's a little early," she said, shutting her ledger book and rising to her feet.

In fact, it was only three p.m. Her brothel, the Jeweled Ladies—one of the finest brothels in the entire state of Texas, if not the entire South—didn't open for business until the evening. Emily kept strict hours in her brothel because it helped secure her position in this town. The doors didn't open until four and they were closed on Sundays.

"There's a girl. You better come."

Emily was already following him down the hall then down the stairs. The large black man was silent as he moved through the brothel. She had fifteen women who worked on their backs for her. True, she had recently lost several girls. She had been running this brothel for close to twenty years now and never had she seen such a spate of whores getting married. Maybe there was something in the water?

Samuel turned at the bottom of the stairs and headed back toward the kitchen. His wife, Della,

1

reigned back here. The Jeweled Ladies was comprised of a saloon that ran along the length of one side of the house and a formal parlor on the other. Behind the parlor was the private dining room. It could be reserved for a price, but mostly it was where the girls took their meals. Della fed all of them as well as serving one hot meal at the saloon every evening. Nobody messed with Della and the kitchen. That woman ruled with an iron rolling pin. A real one.

Samuel pushed open the door and held it so Emily could enter the hot room. Della was in the middle of a full-fledged dinner preparation and the room was swamped with heat and the delicious smell of catfish frying.

But that's not what caught her attention. Her eyes came to rest on a girl. Samuel hadn't been lying. The child could not be more than ten years old. She was grimy looking, with matted hair and rags for a dress. She was standing by the back door of the Jeweled Ladies, shoving Della's cookies into her mouth as fast as she could. There was a tall glass of ice-cold milk next to the cookies and every so often, the girl would pause long enough to take a deep drink.

Emily had not gotten this far in life without being able to see beauty in even the worst of circumstances and the girl was *lovely*. Her skin was light brown, suggesting that she was mixed race. Her hair wasn't tightly kinked, but it wasn't entirely smooth, either. It was the kind of hair that would take a wave beautifully. When she grew up, she was going to break a lot of hearts and looking at her, Emily felt a pang of something that she had long ago decided she wasn't capable of feeling.

If she and Cyrus had ever found a way to be together, this little girl was what their daughter might've looked like.

The moment that thought crossed her mind, she pushed it away. Perhaps in another time or another place... but not here. Not now.

Someone cleared her throat. Emily looked up to Della pointedly nodded off to the side. There was a small table set in the corner of the kitchen where Della sat while she shucked corn or oysters. Emily turned her attention and saw that there was a pile of rags in the chair. As Emily watched, the rags stood and revealed herself to be a black woman whose dress was in even sadder shape than the girl's. "You the madam here?" the woman asked in a rough voice.

"I am Mistress. And whom do I have the honor of addressing?" In addition to having ironclad rules for the Jewels, Emily had ironclad rules for herself. She never treated anyone less because of their age, color, or condition. She may have been raised a lady on one of the finest plantations in Georgia, but she had long ago realized that did not make her better than everyone else.

The woman cackled. She was missing most of her teeth and her skin had open sores on it. Even from across the room, her breath spoke of illness. "I'm Gloria and she's Dolly."

Emily looked back at the little girl. "How do you do, Dolly? My name is Mistress."

The little girl froze in the middle of shoving yet another cookie into her mouth, her eyes wide. Emily wondered if she might bolt. But then Gloria said, "Go on, girl."

3

Dolly swallowed and said, "Is your name really Mistress?" in a tremulous voice.

Gloria moved more quickly than Emily would have given her credit for. In the blink of an eye, she closed the distance between her and the girl and slapped the girl upside the head. "I told you to treat the lady well."

Emily exchanged glances with Samuel. With a sniff, the girl looked up and said, "How do, ma'am."

Emily gave her an encouraging smile. Then she turned her attention back to Gloria, who was shuffling back toward the seat at the table. The woman's appearance was disgusting and her behavior was no better. However, it was clear that the girl was just really dirty. Emily decided to give Gloria the benefit of the doubt. Maybe she had been making sure Dolly had more to eat? "How may I help you today, Gloria?" But she already knew. There was only one reason a woman in such dire straits as Gloria would show up at the back door of the most famous brothel in Texas with a young, terrified girl who had been instructed to treat the lady well.

"She's twelve. She's just small for her age. I figure someone will take her cherry for a pretty penny."

Emily took a deep breath through her nose, keeping her expression blank. The fact was, someone *would* pay a pretty penny for the girl's virginity but it wasn't going to happen here. She may be a whore and a madam but she was not heartless. And even if the girl was twelve, she was still a child, for God's sake.

"I can't get her clean and fed enough that someone would pay me," Gloria went on, oblivious to the stony silence on the other side of the kitchen. Because neither Della nor Samuel were pleased with this offer. "I figure I sell her time to a nice madam like youself and you can get her all fancied up."

Emily didn't have to think about it. If she didn't pay this awful woman for this child, someone else would. "How much?"

Dolly recoiled as if she had been slapped.

Gloria's eyes, however, lit up. "Fifty bucks and she's yours for a month. You'll get your money out of her."

Emily took a step forward. Without even looking, she could feel Samuel and Della closing ranks behind her. They were some of the few people in this world who knew that she was Emily Weatherspoon. The Horners had been with her for decades and if she wanted this horrible woman forcibly removed from her establishment, they would do it without a moment's hesitation. "I'll give you a hundred dollars, but you never get to see her again."

Out of the corner of her eye, Emily could see that Dolly was starting to cry. Tears trickled down her cheeks, cutting a swath through the grime. It hurt to watch, so she didn't. She focused her attention on Gloria. "Do you understand? If I ever see you again, I will not be held responsible for what happens to you. You will never see her, never contact her, and never know anything about her life."

"A hundred dollars?" Gloria rubbed at her cheek, as if she were debating this offer.

Emily was in no mood to negotiate. "Hundred dollars. Take it or leave it." Although this woman was not leaving with this girl.

"You drive a hard bargain but I'll take it."

"You have five minutes to make your goodbyes. Samuel?" Samuel left the kitchen to fetch the money. To a woman down on her luck like Gloria, a hundred dollars was a lot of money. To Emily, it was about fifteen minutes of her evening. "I'll have Della pack you some food for the road. There won't be any need for you to linger in town."

She watched as Gloria crumpled to her knees in front of the girl. "You listen to what the lady says, you hear? She'll take care of you."

"But I don't want to..."

Emily braced for Gloria to slap the child again, but she didn't. Instead, she said, "I know, baby. But I can't keep you. You'll starve to death otherwise. No one will have me. It's the only way."

Emily and Della exchanged glances. Della wrapped up some fresh fried catfish and half a loaf of bread as well as some meat pies left over from yesterday. The bundle sagged under the weight of the food and if Gloria were smart, it might last her a week.

Gloria hugged the girl and Dolly hugged her back. Samuel returned to the kitchen with a hundred dollars in cash.

"That's enough," Emily said. Sometimes, she had to be cruel to be kind. Lingering would do no one any good. The decision had been made and they all had to abide by it.

Gloria got back to her feet, shaking a little. But she took the cash and the food and turned back to the girl. "Love you, baby girl. And I'm sorry. If you think of me, just know that I tried."

The scene would be touching if Gloria hadn't just

sold her daughter. Emily nodded to Samuel, who moved in. "You heard what Mistress said. You be on your way now."

Dolly began to cry in earnest. Emily stepped up and held out her hand. "Come with me, dear," she said in as gentle a voice as she dared in front of Gloria. "Say goodbye."

The girl hesitated and then looked back at Gloria. "Goodbye, Aunt Gloria." Then she put her hand into Emily's.

Emily led her out of the kitchen. To her credit, the girl did not look back. Emily heard the back door shut as the swinging door to the kitchen closed behind them and that was that.

If she ever saw that woman again, there would be hell to pay. It did not matter how dire the circumstances, no one had the right to sell anyone— much less a child. Emily could only thank her lucky stars that Gloria had started with the Jeweled Ladies instead of a less reputable brothel.

Now she was in the possession of a terrified girl. Keeping a firm grasp on Dolly's hand, she led the girl upstairs and then upstairs again, to her private chambers. One of the many advances that the Jeweled Ladies boasted was running water. *Hot* water. It'd cost Emily a small fortune to get pipes run throughout the house, but it was worth it to have hot water for bathing and laundering whenever she wanted.

She had some customers who came solely to take a bath. Oh, sure, they wanted to take that bath with a pretty nude girl, but they were really here for the bath. The girl was just an extra, like sweet icing on a coconut cake.

Dolly was sniffing quietly as Emily closed the door and shot the bolt. "Let's get you into a bath," she said, reaching for the girl's rags. "And I'll get you some new things to wear, lovely and clean." Obviously, she didn't have any children's things in the brothel, but she should be able to get some from the dry-goods store. Even if the Snyders didn't have ready-made clothes, they had five children. They would sell her a dress at an exorbitant mark-up, no doubt, that would fit until something better could be arranged.

The girl burst into tears, racking sobs that nearly doubled her tiny body over.

Emily shifted uncomfortably. Which said something because it took a lot to unsettle her. But she had never been good with small children. She preferred to deal with grown women and men at least sixteen years old, if not older. She wanted people who could make their own decisions of their own free will.

She supposed it could've been worse. She wasn't entirely sure if she believed that the girl was twelve, but at least she wasn't a chubby little toddler. She couldn't abide sobbing. Yet another reason why she had never had her own children. It was just too much. "That's enough of that. You need a bath and a proper meal and probably a real bed."

Dolly straightened back up and tried to stop crying. That was heartening. The girl had gumption. But she was also having a very bad day. "Am I a slave?"

Emily sucked in a pained breath. "Absolutely not. Slavery is illegal in this country. You are your own person and you must never let anyone else make your decisions for you from this moment on. Let's get one thing clear, Miss Dolly. I do not own you. You own yourself. And I will not force you to lie with a man. Your aunt, was she?" Dolly nodded. "Your aunt may have thought that was the only thing valuable about you, but she was wrong. As long as you are under my protection, you will go to school, you will do chores, and you will not give your 'cherry' up to anyone for money. Is that completely understood?"

The girl took a ragged breath, surprise written all over her face. "I'm going to go to school? But I'm colored."

Emily closed her eyes, tamping down her frustration. She had been arguing that colored people should learn how to read and write for almost forty years. It felt like an argument she was never going to win. Her own father had decreed that none of his slaves should read. He believed that most slaves were too ignorant to make sense of letters plus, slaves who could read were dangerous. Emily had never understood how her father could hold two such completely different beliefs at the same time and not see how wrong both were.

So, in secret, she had taught his slaves to read since she'd been old enough to make out the letters herself.

She wished that this were a battle she didn't have to fight. Slavery was now thankfully illegal, but far too many colored people still couldn't read. "You will go to school. We have both colored children and white children in our classroom in this town." She had insisted on an integrated schoolhouse. And her words carried weight in this town.

When she opened her eyes, she saw that Dolly looked worried about this announcement. "This is not a point of negotiation."

There was a knock on the door. She moved Dolly to the side and opened it. Samuel stood on the other side, looking almost as worried as Dolly had. "Everything okay?"

"We're going to need some new clothes. We'll have to burn her things. Surely Mrs. Snyder has something?"

Samuel rolled his eyes. "She's got everything for a price."

But they all had their price, didn't they? "Three dresses and a bonnet. Don't leave without at least two dresses," she added after some thought. She didn't want any of the Snyder children walking around naked because their mother had sold the clothing off their back. "Make it quick. We're supposed to open in a matter of minutes."

Samuel nodded and took off. It was unfortunate that Emily did not have clothing for the child here because Mrs. Snyder would spread word that Mistress had required a child's clothes around town in a matter of hours, if not minutes. But desperate times and all that. "What's your real name?" she asked as she began undressing the girl.

"Dorothea Gibbons. But everyone calls me Dolly."

"Do you know where your parents are?"

She shook her head. "I never knew my pa. My ma worked at a house like this, Aunt Gloria said. But she got sick and died. Gloria cooked in the kitchen because someone knocked her teeth out when she was

10

younger, but we got kicked out because she didn't want to sell me to the madam."

It was taking a great deal of mental energy not to lose her temper. "Where was this?"

"Shreveport."

Emily made a mental note to inquire about madams in Shreveport. She didn't expect her fellow businesswomen to be exactly high in the instep, but there was no need to press a child into the business. "How long have you and Gloria been traveling?"

"We left there a year and half ago. Aunt Gloria says I sing real pretty so sometimes people would give us money for me singing. But not enough."

Emily put all the pieces together. Clearly, Gloria *had* tried but it was hard out there. No one knew that better than she did. She had taken in all kinds of girls in all kinds of desperate straits. "Are you really twelve?"

Dolly's eyes began to water as Emily peeled the last of her clothes off her. The girl was underfed and she had some sores and bug bites on her, but she didn't have any wounds or signs of regular beatings. That had to count for something. "I just turned eleven."

Emily hoped that her hundred dollars was getting Gloria far, far away from Brimstone. Because she would not be held responsible for her actions if she ever saw that woman again.

She drew the bath and added in bubbles because Dolly seemed like she could use a few bubbles right now. She had to cut out some of the girl's hair where the mats had gotten too tangled to brush out. She probably should have left this job for Garnet, but she wanted to keep Dolly hidden—at least until Emily knew what she was going to do with the girl for certain.

The girl was scrubbing her legs when another knock came from her door.

"About time," she whispered to Samuel as he handed her a bundle.

"Mrs. Snyder was in the mood to haggle. Three dresses, two pairs of drawers, an apron, a bonnet, and a pair of shoes."

Emily favored her old friend with a smile. "I forgot about the shoes!"

"I'll make your excuses," Samuel said again as he turned to go.

Emily bolted the door again. The customers were due to start showing up at any moment. Della's catfish brought in almost as many men as the whores did. "I have to get ready for work," she told Dolly as she helped the girl out of the tub and wrapped a thick towel around her. "Samuel brought you some new clothes. I want you to get dressed and I want you to stay in this room. I see you out wandering the halls, I will be unhappy. Do I make myself understood?"

Dolly nodded. Now that the girl was clean, Emily could see that her first instinct had been right. The girl was beautiful. With a little care, she would blossom into a stunning young lady. Because of her light complexion and good hair, she might be able to move between the colored community and the white world a little more easily. Once she got her education, that was.

She cupped the girl's face. "Repeat after me. You are more valuable than your body."

The girl looked sleepy. It had been a long day, no doubt. But she did as Emily bade her. "I am more valuable than my body."

"I'll be back in a little bit with your dinner. After you've eaten, I want you to go to bed. The only person who comes in this room is me. No one else will bother you. In the morning, we will get a better handle on the situation. But I don't want you to be afraid. You are not alone and you're not in danger. You are safe here. Do you understand?"

The girl gave her a watery smile. "Thank you Mistress. I was afraid but I won't be anymore."

"Good girl." Emily patted her on the cheek and then stepped to her dressing table. Normally, she put on quite a great deal of makeup to hide her forty-eight years. But she didn't have time now. She did as little as she could get away with without looking old and compensated by layering on the jewels. The end result was not perfect, but it would have to do.

Dolly watched her silently as she did these everyday tasks. "You really are a fine lady, aren't you?"

Emily smiled at the girl's reflection in her mirror. Dolly looked quite small, dressed in a plain blue dress and curled up in a ball on the top of Emily's wide bed.

"One of the finest." She changed into her heeled slippers and adjusted her bosom for maximum cleavage. "I'm going to lock you in, but don't be afraid."

"I won't be."

Emily was struck with that rare maternal warmth. If only things had been different... But they weren't. So she patted Dolly's cheek again and went down to run her brothel.

Chapter Two

Free Cyrus Franklin sat at the scarred table wedged into his tiny kitchen, staring in shock at the note Isaac had just handed him. He looked up at the silent giant of a man. "Is this true?"

Isaac shrugged. Cyrus had a feeling that the man actually could talk. He just chose not to. His reasons were his own.

"And the letter was just delivered?"

Isaac nodded.

Just to be sure, Cyrus read it a third time.

Mistress bought a girl. Young. She's keeping her at the Jeweled Ladies.

The note wasn't signed.

There had to be a mistake. The woman that the rest of Brimstone knew as Mistress would never buy another person. She especially would not buy a little girl. It went against everything she had ever believed.

At least, it went against everything Emily Weatherspoon believed. But then again, Cyrus didn't know her as well as he once had. He never would've figured she'd have wound up as a madam of a brothel. She'd married a preacher, for God's sake.

Emily Weatherspoon had been the staunchest of abolitionists, a loud voice in the middle of the Deep

South, pushing not just for slaves' rights, not just for colored rights, but also for women's rights. Even Indian rights. Everyone was equal in her eyes. And more than anything, the girl that Cyrus had known abhorred slavery.

He read the note again.

What he needed was more information. There had to be something else in play here. Cyrus couldn't fathom how running a whorehouse had changed Emily over the years. But he couldn't imagine her sinking to this level. She didn't need the money.

Desperately, he wanted to believe that this was an act of goodness and not one of depravity. The Emily he knew would take a girl in and clothe and feed her. The Emily he knew would protect a child from…

Well, from the likes of Mistress, the most famous whore in Texas.

It hurt his heart to think that this could be anything other than a misunderstanding. Mistress was not the same woman he'd known. She refused to give up that brothel of hers. She refused to stop selling girls to men, one hour at a time. She refused to follow the path of righteous honor that she had always insisted she would.

Another thought occurred to him. What if this wasn't just a sign of her slipping further into depravity? What if this was a sign that she was in trouble in some other way? He knew that she was safe in that house of hers, but he worried. He had no right, but he worried anyway. Emily Weatherspoon had made it clear that she was not Cyrus's concern and he was not hers.

Which was all well and good to say, but that didn't make it any less true. No matter how much time had passed or how many miles they'd travelled, he and Emily always seemed to come back to one another.

Just like it did every time he thought of her, Cyrus's body tightened. As Mistress, Emily was one of the finest ladies in town, maybe the state. The clothes she wore put her body to its best advantage. It wasn't the body Cyrus remembered, but it was an amazing body. She made those clothes and jewels look so damn good.

More than once, he'd saddled his horse and stowed some money in a saddlebag, intent on riding to town and buying an hour or a night of her time. Maybe he'd lay her out on her fine bed and plunge his body into hers over and over again until they were both spent and sated. Then he'd take her again, this time, with her on top, riding him wildly, those beautiful breasts of hers freed from their silk trappings for him to touch and suck and bite.

God, there were so many ways he wanted her. She'd been his every fantasy since he'd been old enough to imagine the sexual act as something to enjoy with another person and every day that slipped past with them not talking, not even acknowledging each other, was another day those fantasies burned in a bonfire of frustration.

Those were the bad nights, the ones where his whole body was an instrument of torture that would never seem to end. Taking himself in hand didn't do much but edge the pain back to manageable levels. On the better nights, he saddled up with more honorable intentions. He'd walk into the Jeweled Ladies and pay his money to get her alone and then they'd… they'd talk. They used to talk all the time, when he could slip away from his chores. About nothing and everything. First she'd taught him to read and then she'd snuck him books that she'd already read, so they could debate the finer points of *Ivanhoe* or Shakespeare or the Bible. He'd give anything to just sit next to her, his arm around her shoulder, and have her talk to him like she used to. Had she read Dickens? He thought she'd like Dickens. Or Brontë. Or…

Or anything, as long as they talked. As long as he knew she remembered him.

Either way, with coin in hand, she wouldn't be able to refuse him, would she?

That was the thought that always stopped him cold. He loved her, he lusted after her, he worried about her, but he wouldn't take her if she couldn't refuse him. Thus far, she had refused him completely. The last time he'd seen her across the street, she hadn't even smiled at him. It was almost as if he hadn't been there.

He rubbed his palm over the center of his chest and looked up at Isaac, trying to see what he was missing. "That woman who came through a few days ago… she had a lot of money."

Isaac nodded.

"You think she sold the girl?"

Isaac twisted his face up. Clearly, the man thought it was a possibility.

Damn. Cyrus's place was something of a way station. If the Underground Railroad had still existed, he would be a conductor. But just because that railroad didn't run anymore didn't mean there weren't a lot of people moving around, some who needed a little more help than others.

Cyrus didn't want to go to town. The last time he had done so, he had been arrested on some trumped-up charge and thrown into the lockup before he'd even caught a glimpse of Emily. As night had fallen, he had faced the fact that this could be his end. Black men disappeared all the time. Who would miss him? Obviously, Isaac and all the people who relied on Free Cyrus Franklin's home for a starting place for a better life would note his absence. But none of those people had the power to do anything about him being in jail. The only person who could have helped him was Emily, and as terrified as he had been that his life would be over before dawn, he hadn't been able to bring himself to put her in harm's way.

He knew that people didn't like him. He was a black man who didn't bow and scrape to anyone and a lot of people thought he needed to be put in his place. In the seven years he had lived outside Brimstone, hundreds of people had spent a night or a week or a month at his place and there were plenty of people in town who didn't appreciate the kind of folks who sought him out.

No one had been more surprised than Cyrus had been when the sheriff himself had unlocked the cell door around three in the morning and told him to get out. Even more surprising had been the fact that no one had been waiting for Cyrus outside, ready to make him disappear while leaving the sheriff with clean hands.

Cyrus was not a coward. But he had a healthy respect for the situation and he hadn't been back to Brimstone since. He had no desire to get lynched.

Besides, Emily had made it plain that she did not want to see him. He was nothing but a painful reminder of her past life. He was a threat to her for one reason and one reason alone, he knew who she was. No one else in town knew her name. She was Mistress. She had no past and no future, no history. She existed in the moment. That's what she had said to him when he'd found her.

Not for the first time, he thought about leaving. Brimstone wasn't a safe place for him. Emily wouldn't even look at him. The urge to get out and see the world that, at one time, he had never even known existed was strong. He hated being rooted in one place, feeling trapped and hopeless.

But he hadn't left yet. Not while she was still in Brimstone. Everything he was, every good deed he'd ever done, it was all because of that woman.

He stared at the note again. Everything he was, was because of the woman she had been. Maybe it was time to admit that he didn't know the woman she'd become.

He could not sit by in the safety of the shadows while she sold a child. Either there was something about the situation he didn't know or she needed to be stopped. And, as Mistress, no one could stop her except for Cyrus. She was too powerful.

Really, there was only one thing to do.

"Isaac, saddle up my horse. I'm going to town."

*

At the end of another long but profitable night, Emily looked in on Dolly around three in the morning. She'd gotten into this habit the very first night the girl had been here and even though it'd been a week, Emily seemed helpless to stop.

19

Dolly was curled up into a tight ball in the middle of Emily's bed, visible only because her black hair stuck out against the white silk pillowcases. Dolly didn't stir when Emily closed the door behind her and moved to the edge of the bed.

Emily was not a motherly person. She never had been and the Lord had not seen fit to bless her short marriage to Phineas Weatherspoon with children, a fact for which she daily gave thanks. But looking at this little girl did things to her. Things she didn't like. She felt an overwhelming urge to protect Dolly at all costs. Which was ridiculous.

She cared about all of her girls. She rescued women from desperate straits and gave them choices that they never would have had otherwise. Although everyone seemed to operate under the assumption that every woman who came to the Jeweled Ladies wound up working on her back, in fact the opposite was true. For every Jewel who gave up her name and learned to sell her body for money under Emily's tutelage, there were another four or five who didn't.

Some simply weren't capable of being the refined, beautiful women men paid top dollar for. Like Gloria today, they'd been permanently scarred or otherwise used too hard by life. They couldn't bear to let a man touch them.

Those women chose to be washerwomen or maids or cooks, teachers or governesses. Emily found them positions in good homes or she found them good jobs that would pay them an honest wage they could live on. Emily also found husbands for them, men who needed a farm wife or a mother for their children. Sometimes, she fronted the money so they could open their own shops.

She brushed Dolly's hair back from her face. Dolly sighed in her sleep and Emily was almost overcome with emotion. Her father had sired a few bastards when he'd raped his slaves. Dolly looked like Emily remembered her half-sisters had looked. Junie and Liza—they had been her younger sisters, similar in so many ways, just darker. Emily had shared everything when Emily's parents hadn't been looking. The girls were supposed to be Emily's servants but she had never treated them like that. They were her friends. And against her father's wishes, she'd taught her sisters to read

When her father had found out what Emily had done, he'd sold the girls.

Emily wiped her eyes. It had been a while since she'd tried to find them. Maybe it was time to hire a Pinkerton agent again. Yes, that was a good solution. But she'd no sooner decided on that than another image crowded into her mind, unwanted.

If only she and Cyrus could have found a way… Dolly could have been theirs.

For a moment, she allowed herself to dream of that other life. She and Cyrus would have had to live somewhere remote, where judging eyes wouldn't see a white woman and a colored man living as husband and wife. A plot of land, a family, her sisters if she could find them… they could have been happy. But it would have been a hard life. No hot running water. No fine china, no fine meals. Money would have been tight. They would have been at the mercy of anyone who decided they didn't deserve to live their lives. She would have had to put herself at the mercy of men again and she was *never* doing that.

Dolly sighed in her sleep, burrowing deeper

21

under the sheets. The girl was too lovely by half, but she was not Emily's and she couldn't stay in the brothel. Sooner or later, word would get out that the child was here and Emily didn't want to think who among her clients would suddenly start requesting time with an eleven-year-old.

No, she would not allow it. Anyone who made such overtures would find themselves permanently barred from the Jeweled Ladies. She may traffic in sin, but she would not stand for such evil.

As always, when presented with a problem, Emily began to look for solutions. The girl needed an education. That had to come first. She needed a place to live, too. She couldn't stay here. But that thought filled Emily with such sadness that it caught her off guard. Dolly was such a sweet-looking child. The poor dear had seen a lot in her short life.

Emily shook her head and returned to solutions. As much as she might want to keep Dolly close by, it would not do. But who would take in a colored girl?

She mentally ran through her list of contacts. She had been whoring for almost twenty-eight years now, twelve of them here in Brimstone, and she had built up an extensive list of contacts with other madams, business people, and religious figures that stretched from coast to coast. She could send the girl to San Francisco. She knew a woman there who took in orphaned children. The orphans learned to read and write and were given respectable jobs when they came of age. That would probably be the most reasonable solution. San Francisco was awash in Chinese and Mexicans and colored people. Dolly would blend in there more than she did here in Brimstone.

Or... She could send the girl to Virginia City. One of her former Jewels, now known as Miss Abigail White, was a colored woman who owned her own dress shop. She could teach the girl to sew and become a fine seamstress. Even better, Abigail lived with the former teacher in Brimstone, Miss Minerva Krenshaw. Minerva had come from an abolitionist family and had taught Abigail to read. There, Dolly would be safely coddled by two women who would protect her fiercely. She would get an education and she would learn a respectable trade that would keep her out of brothels.

The more she thought about that, the better she liked the idea. If she sent the girl to Abigail and Minerva, they would send Emily updates. She would know how Dolly was doing. She would know the girl was safe and cared for.

Something in her chest clenched.

It would be enough, she decided. She would write Abigail and Minerva. She would send some money as well. Abigail's shop was quite successful, but she didn't want to put the two women into difficulties.

Silently, she left the room, locking the door behind her again. She would write the letter now. It would be best if she had Dolly away from the Jeweled Ladies as soon as possible. She would need to engage in the services of several Pinkerton agents—to search for her sisters and also to escort Dolly on her way to Virginia City. That way, if her aunt came back, Dolly would be spared the heartache. And more importantly, Emily wouldn't get too attached.

Her mind was restless and her body was tense. Weeks like this made her feel like the weight of the world was upon her shoulders and Emily was wearing down. She couldn't carry it much longer.

She didn't light the lamp in her office. It was pitch black out and one of the reasons her office was in the front of the house was because she liked to look out over the street. Although she held no elected position, Emily considered Brimstone *her* town. She knew almost everyone's secrets. She could exert tremendous control by pulling invisible strings. It was rather amazing how far people would go to keep their secrets quiet.

Emily knew that better than anyone else.

She sat the single candle on her desk and pulled out a fresh sheet of stationary, then set it aside. She needed a clear head before she wrote to Abigail and Minerva, but nothing was clear at this time of night.

Emily pulled a key out from a chain she wore around her neck and unlocked the lower drawer. It'd been months—no, longer than that. Over a year since she'd taken a man to her bed. She no longer needed to whore on an hourly basis and could afford to be particular about the men and women she bedded. But just because she kept her legs closed for business these days didn't mean she wasn't still a woman with needs. So, a few years ago, she'd commissioned a wooden carving from a gentleman who specialized in such... unique sculpture.

Careful not to knock the loaded pistol she kept in the drawer, she pulled a long, thin box out from the drawer and set it on her desk. Her pearl tightened in anticipation of the release as she opened the box and took the carved phallus into her hand. It was a deep mahogany color, almost black in the dim light. The sculptor was a true master of his craft. Emily had several phalluses, including one with an elaborate strapping system that allowed her to wear it and penetrate a man. Those men paid well. She also had one that was a double phallus, one head on each end. Select clientele enjoyed watching two women share pleasure—among other possibilities. Emily was fond of that one. But this dark, wooden cock was her private tool. She ran her hands over the length of the shaft. The sculptor had even worked veins around it, giving it a lifelike feel.

Emily leaned back in her chair and hiked her skirts up. She didn't wear drawers. What whore did? So the only impediment to her access was her corset.

Luckily, she was highly skilled.

She rubbed the wooden cock along the folds of her sex, feeling her juices begin to flow. Then, when she was sure she was wet enough, she plunged the wooden cock into her pussy.

Her time with clients was about pleasure and part of the pleasure was the time leading up until they came in or on her body. Whatever they wanted. But when it was just her, she didn't take her time. She just wanted to get off and get on with her day. Or, in this case, her night.

Her pussy tightened around the wood and Emily stilled her hand, letting her body adjust to the intrusion.

She'd commissioned the piece because she'd grown tired of flesh, of opening herself to others. She'd just wanted to take her pleasure without giving up anything in return. This phallus was one of the best she'd ever owned and she could make herself come within a matter of minutes, but it wasn't the same.

She let her head loll back as she spread her pussy wide with her other hand and located her pearl. Oh, she knew all the words men used for her body and its various parts, but she liked to think of it as her pearl, glowing with her body's cream.

She found the little jewel and began to rub while her pussy tightened and settled around the wooden cock. Her eyes drifted closed as she began to stroke herself in time with the push and pull of the cock inside of her.

And, just like it always did, her thoughts drifted to one man, and only one man. Cyrus's face floated before her and she willed herself to feel his finger on her pearl instead of her own, his cock buried deep inside of her instead of this poor substitute.

She began to writhe in her chair, the springs squeaking as she shifted her hips and plunged the wooden cock into her slick pussy over and over. Cyrus, plunging his warm, soft cock into her over and over. Cyrus, stroking off her pearl. Cyrus, crushing his mouth against hers, the forbidden kiss no longer forbidden.

She threw her head back as her release shuddered through her. Suddenly, the wooden cock was too hard inside of her, buried too deep. She pulled it out, wincing a little. She sat there, her skirts falling back around her waist. She closed her eyes again. The physical release was what she needed but...

She rose and moved to the small washstand in the corner, where she cleaned her phallus and dried it. She returned it to its case and lovingly closed the lid. If only...

She slid the box back into its spot behind the pistol and then she pulled the stationary to her again. With her mind cleared, she knew how to compose the letter to Abigail and Minerva. Yes. This was the right thing to do. Her thoughts were already leaping ahead to the letters she'd send the Pinkerton agency. She'd take out more adverts in newspapers, hoping that Junie and Liza might read them.

But before she put pen to paper, she felt a pull to look outside. Emily had long since learned to trust her instincts on things like that. She blew out the candle and moved to the window.

There was hardly a moon and the street below was thrown into deep shadows. She saw a figure moving along, sticking close to the sides of the building. Intrigued, she studied him. He had a slouch hat pulled low over his eyes but he didn't walk like he was drunk. His movements were careful and deliberate. He made his way along slowly, checking to see that he was not followed.

A spy? She tensed. She may run this town in her own fashion, but that didn't mean she didn't have enemies. She was a sinner and more than a few people wanted to see her gone.

It was probably close to four in the morning now. Her girls had all gone to bed. Samuel and Della were no doubt in bed as well. Emily was just about to step back from the window and get the loaded pistol out of the drawer of her desk when the man stopped in front of the Jeweled Ladies and looked up.

And she knew.

She didn't know *how* she knew. There wasn't much of a moon and the stars weren't putting out a lot of light. The man was still deep in shadows. But she knew it was Cyrus. It had to be. There was something in the way he stood that she would recognize anywhere.

The tightness that had been building in her chest ever since she had paid that woman a hundred dollars for Dolly grew tighter, as if someone was clamping a vice over her heart. She did not like it. Feelings were weakness and, as such, she had made it a policy not to have any. Weakness could be used against a woman to keep her in her place.

That was why she needed to send the girl away.

What was Cyrus doing here? The last time he'd been in town, that she knew of, she'd had to pay the sheriff three hundred dollars to let him go. They had been planning on lynching him and she could *not* let that happen. He had stayed away ever since then and she was glad of it because that meant he was safe. Even if that meant she didn't get to see him, he was safe. That was all she needed.

He took another step out of the shadows and even though she knew that he couldn't see her, his gaze lingered upon her window. Had she called him here with the power of her wishes? Had he finally come to be with her, living flesh instead of hard wood and wisps of dreams? God, how she hoped so. With every fiber of her being, she wanted to go down and throw open the front door and lead him inside. He was here for a reason. She wanted to know that he was well. She wanted…

She wanted things she couldn't have.

She might get that chance, anyway. The damn fool took another step into the street, another step closer to the Jeweled Ladies. Why had he come for her now, after all this time?

Unable to help herself, she touched her hand to the glass.

A gunshot tore through the night.

Chapter Three

Cyrus stuck to the shadows. On the long ride into town made longer because there was no moon out tonight he had run through all the possible outcomes. As Mistress, Emily had finally lost her mind. Maybe she was sick and that was making her do things that she would normally never do. Or, she was keeping the girl safe from something or someone. He didn't know if that was true, but he desperately wanted it to be so. And then there was the third option, one that Isaac had spelled out for him. This could be a trap. But even that very real chance hadn't stopped him. The odds were too great that there was a girl who needed help. Cyrus had helped countless such girls. Girls escaping violent fathers or husbands. Girls forced to do work on their backs in a kind of sexual slavery. Girls who needed to start over for whatever reason.

Cyrus gave them a place to stay and fed them. The ones that needed doctoring, he did the best he could. He buried a few of them. And only very rarely had he ever turned anyone in. He had, though. He did not shelter murderers and rapists. He protected the innocent, not the guilty.

It was the thought of yet another innocent that had him slinking around Brimstone in the dead of night. Well, that and Emily.

The town was quiet. It had to be close to four in the morning. Everyone was asleep. Nonetheless, Cyrus stuck to the shadows.

If Emily had a girl and was planning on selling her for sex, Cyrus had to do something. But what? The former mayor of Brimstone, Raymond Dupree, would have helped him. The mayor's right-hand man, Hank O'Shea, also wouldn't have stood for this injustice. But they had moved on to Austin because Dupree was now lieutenant governor and Cyrus had no such gentlemen's agreement with the current mayor, John James.

Cyrus would have even turned to the old judge, Gerard Hobson, but he was in Austin, too, serving as special counsel to the governor. Hobson was a hard man, but he lived and breathed the law and he would not have allowed Emily to harm a child. Cyrus hadn't heard anything good about his replacement, Aaron Chandler. The man was most likely crooked, which did nothing to make Brimstone a safe place.

Fact of the matter was, Cyrus was more or less on his own here.

He took his time working his way back to Emily's brothel. He could've ridden there in five minutes, but he left his horse outside of town and took the long way around, just in case. If he needed help, he'd have to rely on the churches. He couldn't risk just taking the girl and being arrested for kidnapping. If that happened, he knew his neck wouldn't survive the night, especially if the girl was white.

Finally, he reached his destination. The Jeweled Ladies was dark. The building was huge, and Cyrus understood that Emily had enlarged it over the years. It rose a grand four stories high with a stone face and arched windows. He had never been inside. He wasn't sure he would be allowed in. Every time he had seen her, it had been on the street or at the market.

On two separate occasions, he had helped girls who worked for Emily escape. *Escape* was maybe not the right word. They had wanted to leave but they hadn't felt like they could tell Mistress. One had fallen in love with one of her customers and the other had just realized that she'd made the wrong choice. Cyrus had always heard that Emily would help girls get a new start, but for whatever reason, those girls had come to him and he hadn't turned them away.

Maybe that was why she had refused to acknowledge him the last time they'd passed on the street, right before he'd been arrested.

A light flickered in the second story window and then went out. Was that her? Or was it one of her "girls" finally going to bed after a long night?

Although he couldn't see through the dark windows, he sensed movement and he stepped out of the shadows. He wanted it to be Emily. He was filled with a sudden need to see her, to have her look at him. He needed to know that she remembered who he was—that she remembered who *she* was.

No one lit a light and no one opened a window. But he could feel eyes watching him and it drew him another step into the street. Foolishly, he hoped that the door to the Jeweled Ladies would open and she would be there, hidden by the shadows, beckoning for him.

He heard a click, but it wasn't the sound of a lock. Then an explosion tore through the night and through his back. The pain was overwhelming and he couldn't stay on his feet. Blackness began to pull at him. He struggled to move. He couldn't stay here and wait to be finished off. But nothing worked.

Dammit, it had *been a trap.*

*

Emily stared in horror as Cyrus crumpled in front of her. Two more shapes emerged from the darkness, one of them holding a gun. Trying not to scream, she dug her pistol out of the desk and quietly slid the window up. The two figures stood over Cyrus and to her horror, one of them cocked a pistol.

So she shot him. She shot that son-of-a-bitch and was happy when he cried out in pain before stumbling over Cyrus and falling on his face. She cocked her pistol again and took aim at the second man, but he was already running. Behind her, she could hear thundering footsteps and then Samuel burst into the office.

"Cyrus is shot in the street," she said without looking at Samuel. "Get him inside. I'll cover you."

Samuel turned and pushed back to the crowd of women who were now milling about the hallway, sleepy and scared.

"Mistress?" It was Garnet.

"Be quiet." The man she had shot was struggling to his feet, holding his arm. She thought. It was dark and she could be wrong. She trained the gun on him. She had never personally killed anyone, but she would, to protect Cyrus.

The wounded man stumbled back just as she

heard the front door being opened. A sound that was quickly followed by the distinctive sound of a shotgun being racked.

"Back up," Samuel said.

The man Emily had shot turned and ran.

She kept her gun cocked, though. Just because the two of them were gone didn't mean there wasn't another person watching and waiting. She didn't relax as Samuel scooped Cyrus up into his arms. She didn't see the shotgun, which meant Della was standing in the shadows of the doorway, covering her man and ready to shoot anything that moved.

It wasn't until she heard the front door shut and the bolt hit home that she eased down the hammer on her pistol. As quietly as she could, she closed the window and stuck the gun in the pocket of her dressing gown.

She had a problem. Luckily, she had solutions. "Where's Ruby?"

The girls shuffled and Ruby Red piped up from down the hall, "I'm here, Mistress."

"Do you still have your supplies?"

"Of course."

Ruby was actually Gertrude Kane and she'd worked as a nurse during the Civil War. "Meet me at my room. The rest of you, listen up." Fourteen faces turned to hers, tight with worry. Many of these girls had escaped terrible lives and had no desire to be a part of any violence. "Go back to bed." She looked among her girls before settling on Opal. "If anyone knocks on the front door, Opal, I want you to be wearing your sheerest things. Be ready to make your entrance. The rest of you are going to be asleep. You are exhausted after a busy night and you never heard gunshots. You never saw anything. Do I make myself clear?"

The murmur of voices spoke almost as one. "Yes, Mistress."

"Good. Now go." Thirteen women turned and went. Opal stayed behind. "If anyone comes, I'm counting on you to put on a dramatic performance. Can you do that?"

Opal was Ophelia Simmons and she was an exhibitionist. Most of the time, Emily couldn't even keep a dress on the girl. "I can be nude, if that would help?"

Exhibitionists, Emily thought. "Just have on a dressing gown. Nothing underneath."

Opal nodded and headed back to her room.

Emily shut her office door behind her just as Samuel reached the top of the stairs, Cyrus in his arms and Della trailing after him, shotgun over her shoulder.

"Della, boil some water, but only if you can do so without lighting a candle. Samuel, we're going to take him up to the attic but I need to grab Dolly." If someone came looking, the Jeweled Ladies needed to be *just* a brothel. She could not be harboring a colored man or an orphan girl. Especially not if someone wanted Cyrus dead.

Thank God for the attic. She, Samuel, Della, Pearl and the former Jewel, Sapphire Bleu—now Mrs. Gerard Hobson—and a few select clients were the only ones who knew the attic existed at all. And only she, Samuel and Della knew about the hidden room in the attic.

It was the perfect place to hide a wounded man.

34

Ruby had dressed in a pair of men's trousers and a stained shirt—the clothing she had been wearing when she'd arrived a year ago. She was standing by Emily's bedroom door with her large doctor's bag in her hands. "Obviously, he's been shot," Emily whispered as she unlocked the door.

The girl wasn't in the bed and for a moment, Emily's heart about stopped beating. "Dolly?"

"Mistress?" came a small, terrified voice from the far corner of the room.

She exhaled in relief. The girl had hidden, a smart thing to do, but she'd scared Emily half to death anyway. "Dolly, I need you to come with me right now and I need you to be very, very quiet. Can you do that?"

The girl came out from behind the dressing screen but made a little squeaking noise when she saw the crowd of people. "It's all right," Emily said gently. There was no time for this. "But I need you to come *now*. I need to keep you safe. And they need your help," she added as an afterthought.

Dolly hesitated for only a moment more before she rushed to Emily's side. "We're going to play hide and seek and you and Miss Ruby and Mr. Franklin are going to hide. You need to help Miss Ruby take care of Mr. Franklin, all right?"

By now, they had reached the door to the attic. "Della, lock this behind us and go boil the water," Emily said, leading the way up the pitch-black stairs. Dolly stumbled, but Emily kept a firm grip on her hand.

When they gained the attic, she felt her way to the side table and lit the lamp. This was the room that she used for sadism. It had been empty for a while and it smelled musty. Since Sapphire had married Judge Hobson, she hadn't found another girl who was happy to take the pain and Pearl's services hadn't been requested in some time.

Once the lamp was lit—there was no risk of light being seen from the street below because they had covered over all the windows with heavy layers of blankets to muffle sounds—Emily hurried to the far wall. "Dolly, please help me pull back these blankets."

The girl seemed better now that the lamp was burning brightly. She lifted the blankets back until Emily found the small, nearly hidden keyhole. She unlocked the door that had been built seamlessly into the wall and lit one of the candles. "Ruby, I know it's going to be a tight fit, but see if you can get the bullet out of him. If you hear anything, don't make a sound. Otherwise, don't worry. This room is very well insulated."

If Ruby seemed surprised by any of this, she was doing a good job hiding it. Emily knew she had chosen the right woman for the job. Ruby turned to Dolly and crouched down at her level. "Hi, sugar. Will you help me?"

Dolly looked worriedly at Emily but she nodded anyway.

Samuel carried Cyrus into the small room and laid him on the pallet on the floor. Emily grabbed a few supplies out of the room—blankets, bandages, the salve they used to treat bruises, and stacked them on the narrow shelves that lined one side of the room. Dolly squeezed in by Cyrus's head and Emily said, "Be brave, dear," as Ruby knelt beside Cyrus.

"Save him," she told Ruby, emotion making her throat catch. This wasn't how this was supposed to end. But she didn't have time for useless emotion right now. At any second, the sheriff could come banging on her door and she needed to be ready for him. She turned and saw that Samuel had blood on his shirt. "Get cleaned up and get ready."

The big man nodded and threw one look back at Cyrus before he turned and headed down the stairs.

Emily was set to follow when Ruby said, "You really do have a girl."

"She's not here. Do I make myself understood? She's not one of us."

Ruby shot a look at her over her shoulder. "I'm going to hold you to that."

Just then, Della bustled into the attic, a kettle full of steaming water in her hands. Emily sat it on the shelf next to the candle. Della handed over a bottle of whiskey, as well. "He's going to need this."

Ruby nodded her thanks and Emily said, "Do your best."

It was harder than she thought it'd be to close the door and arrange the blankets so that they looked like they were just part of the wall. It was harder than she expected to pick up the lamp and then lock the attic door behind her. If she only had time, she would've wanted to say something to Cyrus—tell him to hold on, tell him that she would keep him safe, tell him...

She locked the door at the bottom of the attic stairs and hurried back to her office. She could still smell the acrid scent of gunpowder, so she went to her room and grabbed a bottle of her French perfume. This was a whorehouse, after all. It might as well smell like one.

Then she stood at the window and watched the street. At some point, Samuel poked his head back in. "Opal is going back to bed, but she's ready if you need her."

"Did you get rid of your shirt?"

"Burned it in the furnace. You think they'll come after him?"

"Yes." Now that the immediate danger was passed, exhaustion began to tear at her. "What was he doing here, Samuel?"

"Don't know. But he's here now."

She didn't say anything. She turned her attention back out the window, watching for any sign of the sheriff or a posse. "Will you keep watch?"

"I'll be in the parlor."

"Thank you, Samuel."

"Emily?"

She winced at the name. It was so rare to hear it spoken out loud. "Yes?"

"He'll be all right."

Stupid emotion clogged up her throat again and her eyes began to sting. "That will be all, Samuel."

The door clicked behind him, and just like she always was, Emily was once again alone.

*

Searing pain ripped through Cyrus's back and he screamed. The pain cut through the blackness that seemed to be holding him down.

"Sugar? I want you to fold up that towel and put it in his mouth. Be gentle."

"I don't want to hurt him," came a smaller, more scared voice and dimly, Cyrus thought, *it's the girl.*

38

"You won't. Now do as I say. That's a good girl."

A rag was shoved into his mouth. Cyrus tried to spit it back out, but he didn't have the strength. Then another searing pain shot through his back and he tried to flail.

"Don't cry, sugar. If he can scream, he's still alive. And that's a good thing."

He was still alive. That had to count for something.

"I want you to hold the candles so the light is focused—yes. You are a very good helper. What's your name?"

"Dolly."

Somehow, Cyrus managed to get the rag out of his mouth. "Emily."

"Who?"

"Emily…" The pain was so much that he started to drift back into the darkness, where he didn't hurt.

He was going to die and he hadn't even gotten to see her again. Everything he was, was because of her.

"Is that your sweetheart? I don't know an Emily."

She had so many names. He knew she did. But he could only think of one. "Franklin. Emily Franklin."

"She sounds very pretty," the voice said gently.

It wasn't Emily, damn it all.

"This is going to hurt. Dolly, sugar, why don't you put that towel back in his mouth again and then I'm going to need you to hold his head still. I've got to get this bullet out of him."

Cyrus tried to turn his head, but whoever Dolly was, she wasn't taking *no* for an answer. Then there was another searing pain and it just kept coming in waves and he let himself slip beneath the blackness

39

where things didn't hurt and Emily Franklin was the most beautiful girl he'd ever kissed.

*

Emily didn't have to wait long. At five thirty, a man holding a lantern worked his way down the street. He stopped in front of the Jeweled Ladies and stared at the bloodstained street. In an exhausted daze, Emily watched as the man tilted his head down and stared at the dirt. Then he looked up at the brothel.

It was Sheriff Cutler. She didn't know if that was a good thing or not.

Emily knew she looked like hell and normally, she would never let anyone see her in this state. But right now, it was working for her. She may not have made it to bed tonight, but she certainly looked like someone had gotten her out of one.

She watched as Sheriff Cutler moved toward the brothel. When he disappeared from view, she waited until she heard the knock on the door. Then she went down the hall to Opal's door and knocked softly.

She could hear Samuel and the sheriff talking. Samuel had his voice pitched up loud, to make sure that she could hear him, no doubt. But neither of the voices sounded angry. This was probably the best possible outcome. Someone had heard the shots and woke up the sheriff and he had come to see if there were any bodies. Sheriff Cutler was usually a reliable officer of the law. Emily would rather take her chances with him than with a posse.

The door opened and Opal blearily peered out, pulling her dressing down around her bare shoulders.

"I'm going to go downstairs. Count to one hundred and then stumble downstairs," Emily whispered, close to Opal's ear. "You're a light sleeper, remember. You heard a noise outside, and you went to check, but you didn't see or hear anything."

Opal nodded and closed the door to a crack.

Emily went to the top of the stairs and listened. She heard Samuel say, "Everyone's asleep here," and she heard Sheriff Cutler reply, "All the same, I'd like to talk to Mistress."

That was her cue. She moved down the stairs less gracefully than she might normally. She wanted Sheriff Cutler to believe that she had stumbled out of bed. "Samuel? What's going on?"

Samuel turned, looking just as exhausted as she was. "Sheriff said there was a shooting in the street sometime after we closed last night."

Emily blinked several times, allowing shock to register on her face. "There was a shooting?" She stepped around Samuel and addressed herself to Sheriff Cutler. "Was anyone killed?"

The room was in long shadows from the sheriff's lantern. Samuel lit the lamp and Emily said a prayer for her wounded pride because when the sheriff looked at her, his eyes got wide as his head jerked back. Oh, this would be the talk of the town for a while. The sheriff had seen her without her makeup on.

But as long as it served to distract him from searching the building it was a sacrifice her pride was happy to make. She turned the Samuel. "My bedroom is so far away from the street. Did you hear anything?"

He shrugged. "I just thought it was some drunks in the street. I didn't pay no mind to it."

41

She could always count on Samuel. She turned back to the sheriff. "I'm sorry, Sheriff Cutler. Samuel's bedroom is closest to the front door. If he didn't hear anything…"

Timing was everything and Emily had rigged the timing in this particular situation because right then, Opal sleepily strode into the room, stretching her one arm over her head. She was completely nude underneath her dressing gown—which hung open and off one shoulder. "What's going on? I'm trying to sleep. Oh!" she exclaimed when she registered the Sheriff's presence. One hand fluttered over her bare breast. "Why, Sheriff Cutler. I didn't realize you were here."

Emily shot the girl a look. There was no need to lay it on so thick. "Opal, dear, would you tie your dressing gown, please?"

However, when it came to Opal, laying it on thick was the only way she worked. She looked down at her naked front and said, "Oh. Oh! How *silly* of me. I'm so sorry, Sheriff Cutler." Then and only then did she pull the sides of the dressing gown together and knot the belt.

Sheriff Cutler cleared his throat. "Morning, Miss Opal."

"Opal, what are you doing out of bed?" Emily yawned for emphasis.

"I heard voices. You know I'm such a light sleeper, Mistress." She turned to the Sheriff and gave him a sleepy smile. "I always have been."

Sheriff Cutler cleared his throat again. "Miss, we had some reports of gunshots this morning around four. Did you hear anything?"

Opal appeared to think about it. "Why, I did. I even got up to make sure that it wasn't inside. You know Mistress has rules about guns in the building."

Sheriff leaned in, paying close attention. Emily prayed that Opal wouldn't overplay her hand. "And what did you see?"

Opel batted her eyes. "I saw some men in the street. But they were just moving on. I didn't think anything of it. I had a long night and I was tired." Her voice descended into a pout and she stretched like a cat again, which make the dressing down gape at the chest. "Can I go back to bed now?" Before anyone could answer her, she took two quick strides over to where Sheriff Cutler was standing. She looped her arms around his neck and said, "You could come with me."

Sheriff Cutler looked shocked as Opal nuzzled him, her head on his shoulder. His arms moved and for a moment, Emily thought that Opal had worked her magic and that she was about to take the sheriff to bed. Which was not actually what she wanted, because that meant the sheriff would still be in the building and it would be difficult for her to go up and check on Cyrus and Dolly and Ruby. She needed a few hours without anyone in this house.

But Sheriff Cutler merely grabbed Opal's wrists away from his neck and sat her off to one side. "A tempting offer, but there's a fair amount of blood in the street and I need to figure out who shot who."

Opal pouted. "It was dark out and I was sleepy. I just saw two men walking down the street. I couldn't see anything else."

"And there was no one lying in the street?" Sheriff Cutler's question set Emily's teeth on edge.

Why couldn't it have rained and washed out the signs of struggle? If he had deduced that there had been a body lying in the street, then he also might have seen Samuel's footprints going out of and back into the Jeweled Ladies. Dammit.

Opal shook her head.

Sheriff Cutler gave her a long look but Opal just smiled. "Thank you for your time, Miss Opal."

"I'm happy to give you anything you want, Sheriff. Come by and see me sometime." With a sly wink, she turned and waited for Emily to dismiss her.

"That will be all, Opal. Thank you for your help."

With a yawn that did not seem faked at all, Opal headed for the stairs. She wasn't even out of the room before she untied the dressing gown and slipped it off her shoulders.

Exhibitionists, Emily thought with a barely contained smile as Sheriff Cutler cleared his throat again.

She turned back to the man. "I'm sorry we can't be more helpful, Sheriff Cutler. But my girls worked late last night and I'm sure that everyone else is fast asleep." At least, they better be.

The sheriff looked from Samuel to Emily and back again, as if he were trying to decide if they were being truthful or not. "I'm sorry to disturb you. But if anyone should let something slip to one of your girls about a gunfight…"

"Of course," Emily volunteered. "I prefer to keep guns out of Brimstone entirely. Dead men don't pay for women."

Sheriff notched an eyebrow at her. He really was a handsome man, though not one who frequented her establishment. Although after that performance by Opal, who knew? "Some of us don't pay for women at all, Mistress. But I thank you for your time."

She nodded and stood in the parlor while Samuel showed him the door. She needed to check on Cyrus and Dolly. Hopefully, that man hadn't done anything ridiculous like die on her. She wasn't sure she could trust herself to rush up to the attic right now. She wouldn't put it past Sheriff Cutler to 'suddenly remember' something he wanted to ask and knock on the door in another fifteen minutes, just to make sure they weren't doing something nefarious.

Ten minutes. She went to the kitchen and put the water on. She needed a cup of tea and she needed to take fresh water upstairs, in case Ruby needed it.

As she waited for the water to boil, her mind tried to find some solutions to this problem. Having Cyrus in the house made everything a million times more complicated. It was bad enough that she had Dolly here, worse that Ruby had heard rumors about it.

For all of her wealth and power, Emily knew exactly how tenuous her position in this community was. She was tolerated because she offered a service in high demand. Her power came from knowing nearly every peccadillo of the men, and more than a few of the women, in town. On their own, no single person could remove her. But if the powers that be were to find a single cause they could unite behind...

Unconsciously, she put a hand to her throat as the kettle began to whistle. There were too many people in this town who would sleep better knowing that their secrets were no longer held by Mistress of the Jeweled Ladies.

She didn't bother to check the time. She did check the parlor again, where Samuel was sitting up in the bow window, watching the street through heavy eyes. "Anything?"

He shook his head.

"I'm going to check on them. Try to get some sleep."

He snorted as if she'd told a joke.

Climbing up to the attic was a long process when one was holding a kettle of boiling water. Carefully, Emily unlocked the attic door and then relocked it behind her. She sat the kettle down at her feet and felt her way along the walls. She shouldn't have carried the lamp down earlier, but she hadn't wanted to leave it up here, proof of having recently been lit, just in case the sheriff had demanded to search the house.

Eventually, she found the right spot on the far wall. She lifted the blankets away enough to gently knock on the door. There was a nervous squeak from the other side and then Ruby said, "Mistress?"

"It's me. But I don't have a light."

The door pushed open and candlelight spilled out onto her. Dolly was curled into an impossibly small ball near Cyrus's head, fast asleep. Cyrus was on his stomach, seemingly not dead. At least, she hoped that was his chest rising and falling. It could be the candlelight playing tricks on her.

Her chest clenched at the sight of his back. Ruby hadn't been able to get his shoulder properly bandaged—obviously, there had been no way for her to raise Cyrus up enough so she could wrap a bandage around his chest. The nasty-looking gunshot wound on his right shoulder had been neatly sewn back up and the area cleaned, but it still looked ghastly.

And around it...

Ruby had cut away some of Cyrus's shirt, leaving his back exposed. Scars crisscrossed his back in such number that it was impossible to distinguish where one scar started and the next ended.

Old scars. *Whipping* scars.

Emily's stomach turned as a memory as old as the scars fought its way to the surface.

He'd kissed her.

No, that wasn't an accurate statement—she had kissed Cyrus. She'd been fourteen and upset about her sisters and gone running into the woods, to their secret spot. And he'd found her some time later and put his arm around her shoulders and held her while she'd cried until she had no tears left. But he hadn't stopped holding her and as the seconds blurred into minutes, the space between their bodies had gotten smaller and smaller and she'd been possessed with this unnatural urge to kiss him, to bury the betrayal she felt at the fact that her father would sell his own daughters, her only sisters, underneath a new emotion she hadn't been able to name then.

She had a name for it now. Lust. Desire. *Want.* She'd wanted Cyrus, wanted the balm that he could provide for her soul. Even at fourteen, she'd hated having emotions. Hated being weak and powerless.

So she'd taken what little power she'd had, her control over her person, and pressed her lips to his. After only a painful moment's hesitation, he'd kissed her back. A long, leisurely kiss that went on and on, tongues and mouths exploring and tasting and discovering that what she'd always felt for Cyrus was only the very beginning of what she could feel.

She had never quite figured out if someone had seen them or if her father had just guessed. Emily hadn't been the master of dissembling then that she was now. Had her father seen the truth of knowledge and happiness on her face? Or had one of his spies finally found their secret spot?

It didn't matter, not in the end. In the end, her father had done this to Cyrus.

And Cyrus had told Emily that it'd only been a few lashes, nothing bad. Nothing she had to worry herself about.

He'd lied, she realized as she pushed aside the tattered remains of his blood-soaked shirt to reveal even more knotted scar tissue. All those years ago, he'd lied to her. Why? What had he hoped to gain by protecting her father? The man did not deserve Cyrus's protection, just as he had never deserved Emily's love or devotion.

"Oh," she whispered, kneeling in the narrow doorway, her hand fluttering above his back. Reasonably, she knew that the scars were old and no longer stung. But she was afraid to touch them anyway. After hesitating for a moment, she instead put her hand on Cyrus's head.

"He's still alive," Ruby said, exhaustion heavy in her voice as she leaned against the far wall.

Emily startled at her voice. She'd been so riveted by Cyrus's back that she had forgotten there was someone else in the room. And it was a very small room.

"He lost a lot of blood and we'll have to work hard to make sure he doesn't get an infection. Hopefully, the carbolic acid will do the trick." She held out a bloody wad of cloth. "But the bullet was intact and it wasn't very deep. He got lucky. Missed everything important."

Emily hoped as well. As she watched, Cyrus's back rose and fell in a steady rhythm. Definitely not a trick of the light. "Sheriff Cutler came by. I'm not sure he believes that no one saw anything, but he left."

Even though he was unconscious, Cyrus's head rolled into her palm.

Tears pricked at her eyes. It had been so long…

"He kept asking for someone," Ruby said. "Someone named Emily—Emily Franklin? I hadn't heard that he was married."

Emily tensed. On the verge of death, leave it to Cyrus to remember *that*. She hadn't been Emily Franklin for decades. "I'm sure it was nothing."

She backed out of the room so Ruby could stand and stretch. Her clothes were covered with fresh bloodstains. "I don't suppose I can convince you to burn those?"

Ruby shook her head. "Always have an escape plan, Mistress. Mine happens to involve pants."

Emily might have argued with her any other day, but they were all tired. "Get some sleep. I'll stay with him. But Ruby, no one else knows about this room. No one."

Ruby stepped out of the narrow room and paused, her doctor's bag in hand. "Does anyone else know about the girl?"

"Just Samuel and Della. I'm not keeping her," she defended before Ruby could make a statement. "She doesn't belong here. I'm going to send her to Abigail in Virginia City. Far, far away from here."

"Good. We heard a rumor that you bought a girl and we were worried."

Emily looks back to the unconscious girl curled a ball near Cyrus's head. "I gave her aunt money to leave. Otherwise, that woman would have sold her to someone else and I couldn't stand by while that happened."

Ruby exhaled in obvious relief. "She's a good girl. Didn't cry or anything."

"Get some rest."

With a nod, Ruby left. Emily got up and locked the attic door behind her and then carried the kettle of water back to the closet.

She settled on the floor by Cyrus, filling her eyes with him. She had wanted to see him again, but not like this. "You had to go and ask for Emily Franklin, didn't you," she teased, because it was that or cry and she hadn't cried since the day she'd kissed Cyrus. Not the day her husband had been killed, nor the dark days that had followed.

She poured some of the hot water onto a clean cloth. She let it cool in her hands for a few moments before she began to wipe it over his face. Ruby had done a good job getting the blood cleaned off his back, but there was still dirt on his face and she didn't like it. "Don't you dare die on me, Cyrus. I couldn't bear it."

He sighed in his sleep and that made her feel better. She made sure the blankets were flat and then closed the door and blew out the candle. A warm darkness settled over the small room. Emily lay next to him, her hand resting on top of his, and fell asleep.

Chapter Four

Cyrus's eyes fluttered open, but that didn't change the view. There was nothing but stark blackness and he wondered for a second if he was actually dead. Or maybe he was just in limbo? That was a distinct possibility. Wherever he was, it wasn't Heaven.

He tried to move as an experiment of sorts. Pain rippled through his back and he gasped, which made someone else gasp.

"Cyrus?"

Emily. "If you're here, that either means we're both dead or..." If they were dead, that was a damned shame, but then, they were apparently dead together and that was a comfort.

"How can you joke at a time like this? You damn fool. Don't move," she said more forcefully. "I need to light the candle."

He didn't enjoy being bossed around, but the one movement had hurt, so he lay there while she fumbled. He didn't know where he was but it didn't matter, did it? Emily was here, as if he had called her out of the dream.

He hadn't ruled out being dead.

A match flared then a candle threw light into what turned out to be a small space. He lifted his head to look around. He wasn't in his house. "Emily?" The words felt thick on his tongue.

"I'm here." She knelt beside him and lowered her head so that she could look him in the eyes. She pressed a cup to his lips and water dripped into his mouth.

That was when he decided that he wasn't really dead because if he were, Emily would look like she had thirty years ago, back when she had been the prettiest flower in all of Georgia. Instead, she looked her age. She was still the most beautiful woman he'd ever seen. He wanted to reach out and touch her, to make sure she was real. But when he tried to lift an arm, that pain shot through him again.

"What happened?"

She sat back on her heels, frowning at him. This was the Emily he knew now—hard and disproving. "You're in the attic of the Jeweled Ladies. For some fool reason, you came into town last night. I was in my office and I saw someone slinking through the shadows. It was you and then someone shot you in the shoulder. Two men, one with a pistol. I wounded the one with the gun and Samuel carried you inside."

Ah, he remembered now. "I heard you had a girl."

The words took a lot out of him, but he didn't miss her reaction. Her frown deepened until she was outright scowling at him.

"And you assumed I would... What? Sell her virginity to the highest bidder?" She made a noise of disgust. "Really, Cyrus."

"How was I supposed to know?"

He wasn't making things better. If he weren't in so much pain, he would be tempted to laugh at her.

52

Her face was screwed up into a mask of righteous indignation. She had always been prone to righteous indignation. "Do you have so little faith in me?"

His eyes drifted shut. "I was worried about you. Thought if you were going to sell a girl, there had to be something wrong with you. Needed to see... With my own eyes." Eyes that were suddenly heavy.

He heard Emily sigh with exasperation. "Now you're going to fall back asleep and leave me with that parting shot, I suppose? What am I supposed to do with you, Cyrus?"

He was already starting to float. "You could always marry me."

He felt her fingertips stroking over his forehead. Her touch warmed him from the inside, a good heat. "Oh, Cyrus. I wish..." But she didn't finish the sentence. "Rest now."

He didn't want to rest. He hadn't talked to her— really *talked* to her—in so long that he didn't want to waste a single moment of their time together.

But he didn't have a choice. He slipped off into the darkness. All he could do was hope that she would still be there when he woke up.

She wasn't. Cyrus came awake from a dream of his limbs entwined around Emily, her body pressed against his. A noise. There was some noise that pulled him out of the dream before he could enjoy himself properly.

It took him what felt like years to get his eyes open. The room was empty. Lit, but empty.

He managed to get his left arm underneath him but his right wasn't working. Somehow, he pushed himself up into a sitting position and looked around. This small room was stocked with provisions and candles on the shelves. Where was he? This was not the kind of room that a brothel would have. At least, he didn't think it was.

In all honesty, this was more like the room he had in his home—small and cramped and hidden. A place where someone who needed to hide could stay for a few days. Was it a holdover from the Underground Railroad?

Cyrus took stock. He hurt like hell but he figured that was a good thing. If he had gone to the great hereafter, surely he wouldn't be in this much pain.

There it was again, a noise from outside this tiny room. He could see a door now, a little crack in the wall. If it weren't for the handle on the crack, he wouldn't have guessed there was a door at all. This was a good room. Safe. He'd stayed in far worse during his time.

He shifted his legs and nudged the door with his foot. It didn't move very far, almost as if there was something resting against it on the other side—but it moved enough. A few minutes later, the door eased open and a little colored girl's face peered in at him.

The girl. He was in a safe place and the girl was here with him. He'd been shot but Emily… Where was Emily?

"Morning," he said, his voice dry and scratchy. How long had he been asleep?

She shot him a nervous smile. "It's after lunch," she informed him in a matter-of-fact tone. "You want some water? Miss Ruby said I should give you some if you woke up."

Cyrus hadn't realized how thirsty he was. "Yes, please."

The little girl stepped into the room and the door softly closed behind her—but not all the way. It stayed open a crack. "We're supposed to stay up here," she went on in that matter-of-fact tone that Cyrus had learned children developed when they'd seen more than they should've. "If I hear anyone at the door, I'm to come in here with you, shut the door and blow out the light so that we aren't found."

She held a cup up to his lips and Cyrus drank deeply. He stopped when his stomach turned. Too much, too fast. He leaned his head back against the wall and breathed deeply until his stomach settled. "Who's looking for you?"

"No one. At least," she went on, giving him a shy smile, "I don't think anyone's looking for me, but Mistress is worried. She doesn't want anyone to know I'm here."

"Why not?" That was a good thing, right? If Mistress were going to sell this girl, she would be advertising it in the paper.

The girl sat on her heels and twisted her face up, as if she were thinking real hard. "I know what kind of place this is. My ma worked in a place like this. My aunt Gloria was a cook in a place like this, too. Mistress says that I am not to be bought and sold. I am my own person and I have more value than my body?" She finished like she'd tried to memorize a lesson and wasn't sure if she'd gotten all the words right.

The relief was even sweeter than the water had been. Emily was still Emily. Thank God above. "What's your name?" As he asked, the name Gloria rattled around in his head. He was more sure than ever that that had been the name of the woman who had passed through—when was it? He had no idea how long he'd been here.

"Dolly. Dorothea," she corrected, "but everybody calls me Dolly, because I look like a little doll."

"Dolly," he repeated, making sure the name stuck. His mind wasn't working quite like it should, but then again, he had been shot, so perhaps that was understandable. "My name is Free Cyrus Franklin," he told her, lifting his good arm. It wasn't the right hand for shaking, but she squeezed his fingers anyway. "Pleased to make your acquaintance."

The effort took a lot out of him and he leaned his head back against the wall, his eyes closed and his stomach still turning. He might've dozed, because when he opened his eyes again, Dolly was gone. The door was still open a crack, which he took as a good sign. No one had found them yet.

He drifted again, trying to get his mind to answer the question of what would happen next. He was locked in the attic with a girl Emily was trying to hide but everyone knew was here, anyway. He'd been shot by someone. Emily and someone named Miss Ruby had stitched him up, he was pretty sure. Surely, he concluded, Emily hadn't been the one to set the trap. She hadn't sent the note. She hadn't known he was coming.

A new, terrible thought startled him so much that he accidentally kicked the door. His home. Isaac, and Beulah and Rob Boy—they were the only two people staying at the house, but they'd been down in the cellar while Rob Boy recovered.

Dolly peered back into the room. "You all right?"

"I need to talk to Mistress or this Ruby lady. Can you get them for me?" He wasn't too worried about Isaac. The big man could take care of himself. But Rob Boy had been whipped mighty hard and if the house burned down on top of him, he and Beulah would have no way out of the cellar.

"We're locked in and I don't have a key."

Cyrus felt that muscle in his jaw clench. There was a part of him that rationalized that Emily was only trying to keep him and Dolly safe but oh, he hated to be locked up anywhere. He'd been a freeman longer than he'd been enslaved, and his freedom was *everything*.

"Do you want more water?" Dolly asked. She sounded worried.

Cyrus exhaled slowly, letting go of the anger. A level head was required here. Getting mad would only upset the girl. He would have to wait until someone came to check on them. "Can you help me up?"

Dolly looked doubtful, but she took hold of his good arm and helped pull him to his feet. He got his feet underneath him and Dolly led him out into the room.

It was not a bedroom. It had what looked like castoffs from someone's parlor furniture—a large ottoman, a wingback chair, and the settee. There was a cabinet in the corner and the table next to the settee. And that was it except for the blankets hanging from all the walls.

They made their way over to the settee where he sat, sweating with the effort. Dolly got him another drink of water but before he could enjoy the cool

57

drink, the sound of a key turning a lock came from somewhere in this room. He couldn't see where.

Dolly squeaked and dove behind the wingback chair as the door opened. "Easy, sugar," came a warm female voice that sounded vaguely familiar. "It's just us."

"Is he up?" came a much more familiar voice. Emily.

Cyrus stared, unsure if he was dreaming or awake. A gorgeous woman with russet-red hair and a gown the exact same color swanned into the room. One of Mistress's Jewels, no doubt. And behind her...

His breath caught in his lungs. Emily looked like... well, like Mistress. She was not the fresh-faced girl of his memory, but the grown woman he'd seen about town. Her gown was of peach silk so luminous it glowed and her neck and ears glittered with gems. She was a proper lady and completely improper all at the same time and he'd never been so glad to see her.

"He is," the Jewel said.

Emily stepped into the room and sniffed, her nose wrinkling in distaste. "Well, that settles it," she said, dusting off her hands. "Dolly, come along. It's time to leave the attic. Mr. Franklin will not tolerate being locked up like a common criminal and you need to have your own room. Although it'll only be for a few more days, we have one ready for you right next to Miss Ruby's, but no one else will have entry except for her and me. Is that all right?"

He grinned at her. Dear God in Heaven, she remembered him. How had he ever thought she'd forgotten him? Emily didn't talk to him, though. She didn't even look at him.

Dolly thought that over. "Do I get a window this time?"

"Yes, dear girl." To Cyrus's amazement, Emily smiled at the girl. It was full of warmth and something else, something he couldn't quite name. "But you'll still need to stay inside for a while longer."

Cyrus frowned. There was something he needed to ask… "Isaac?"

"Who's that?" the Jewel asked. She walked right over to Cyrus and put her hands on his body, leaning him forward. "Hmm, no sign of infection," she murmured, her cool hand stroking over his wound.

"Thank God for that," Emily sighed. "Who's Isaac, Mr. Franklin?"

Cyrus scowled at her. Why was that woman calling him Mr. Franklin? "My friend. Lives with me."

"This Isaac got a last name?" the Jewel asked. He could feel her hands pressing and puckering his skin.

"No. I got a note. It was a trap. They might have burned me out." The Jewel leaned him back and he could look at both the women again. "I had two people hiding." He swallowed, his mouth already dry. "How long?"

"Two and a half days." Emily was looking hard at him. "This complicates things mightily. If it was a trap—"

"It was," Cyrus and the Jewel said at the same time.

"Then the brothel is probably being watched," she finished as if they hadn't interrupted her.

"I can go. They won't recognize me. I'll slip out this evening after the first wave of gentlemen callers," the Jewel said.

Cyrus couldn't imagine how anyone wouldn't recognize the Jewel. She was striking and tall and fine-boned. But Emily nodded. "Did your guests have names?"

59

"Beulah and Rob Boy. He was hurt. In a cellar. Door under the chair in the parlor. Don't want them to die on my account." At this point, Cyrus didn't have a choice. He normally never told anyone but Isaac about who he was sheltering. But there was no way he could do anything.

"I'm definitely going," the Jewel said. "Let's get you downstairs, Mr. Franklin."

"We haven't been properly introduced." It was a faint stab at civility, but it was the best he could do. "I'm Cyrus Franklin."

"Gertrude Kane. But call me Ruby—everyone here does."

Of course they did. Ruby turned to Dolly. "Sugar, can you help Mistress and I get Mr. Franklin downstairs? Then you and I can check out your new room."

The girl blushed, looking pleased. "Yes, Ma'am."

Ruby and Emily lifted him up, with surprising strength from Ruby, and they each tucked under one of his arms. Cyrus barely had to walk to the door.

Somehow, they made it down the stairs and to the room at the far end of the hall. His legs functioned, but the way Ruby was hefting him about sent spikes of pain down his back, which made his legs feel like they were operating out of rhythm, like he was a newborn colt trying to get his feet under him.

The women ushered him through what was clearly a bedroom but he didn't get a good look at it. All he got were impressions—peach and gold and, oddly, bright blue. Clean, tasteful. Emily and Ruby carried him through a side door and it took Cyrus a moment to realize what he was looking at.

It was a huge bathing tub, the kind with claw feet, long enough for a man to soak his whole body in.

He wanted to protest as Ruby held him up and Emily stripped his tattered shirt off. He didn't want them to look. He couldn't bring himself to care if Ruby saw the scars, but God help him, he didn't want Emily to see his back. Not that.

"No," he protested, but it came out weakly.

"Yes," the women agreed in unison.

"Mr. Franklin," Emily went on, that severe politeness in her voice, "this is a clean house. We cannot have guests smelling like a prison hospital ward." With that, she stripped him down to his smallclothes.

"Nothing we haven't seen before," Ruby added, sounding amused. "And, seeing as I'm the one who stitched you up, none of this is particularly new to me." She plucked the strings of his smallclothes and that was how Cyrus found himself buck naked before two of the prettier women in Texas with the complete absence of a hard-on.

But he didn't have the strength to argue or protest when the two women unceremoniously lowered him into the tub. This was fine. He was wounded but they were taking care of him. The water was warm and covered him and he wasn't standing anymore.

But that wasn't the most important thing. The most important thing was that Emily had been at his front. She hadn't seen his back. And now that he was in the tub, it could stay that way.

"You're healing well, Mr. Franklin," Ruby said as the warm water enveloped him. "But you'll need to take it easy for a few more days. I'll check on your friend."

Cyrus had no idea how she would be able to pull that off, but more power to her. "Much obliged."

Ruby turned her attention to Emily. "Mistress, after he's done—"

"Yes, of course." Emily was staring down at him with something that might have been tenderness on another woman. It still looked stern on her, though. "Leave the supplies, then see to Dolly. And do let me know before you leave."

"Yes, Mistress."

Then she was gone. The outer door clicked and Emily disappeared. He heard another lock click and he knew they were well and truly alone.

The trip down the stairs had taken a lot out of him and the warm water felt like heaven. He was content to stay here forever.

He heard rustling and then footsteps. When he managed to get his eyes open again, Emily was standing before him in her shift and corset.

"You," she said in an imperious tone as his mouth fell open, "need a good scrubbing."

"I do seem to find myself in a tub. Leave some soap and I'll…"

Before his eyes, she unlaced the corset. It was pink and embroidered with delicate swirls of lace pinned to the edges.

Then it fell away and his breath caught in his throat. "Emily, what are you doing?" It came out strangled sounding.

She looked at him as if he'd asked what color the sky was. "Why, Cyrus—isn't it obvious? I'm giving you a bath."

Chapter Five

During her time, Emily had stripped down for more men and women than she could count. So there shouldn't have been anything erotic about this particular disrobing.

Except this wasn't a paying guest. This was Cyrus. And he was looking at her with a mixture of confusion and something else.

Want. Bless the man, he still wanted her.

"You—" his voice gurgling like he'd been shot in the chest instead of the shoulder. "You can't."

If she was hurt by that refusal, she didn't allow herself to feel it. "I fail to see how you're going to wash yourself, Cyrus. As best I can tell, you can't exactly use your right arm and you and I both know you're right-handed."

The color on his cheeks deepened. "You remember that?"

She put her hands on her hips and sighed dramatically. He still had his stubborn streak, too. "You think I'd forget?"

He rested his head on the back of the tub, but he was watching her underneath his thick lashes. "Sure seemed like you forgot for the last few years."

If anyone else were in her tub, she'd simper and

smile and make him forget he'd said anything at all. But this wasn't any man.

Already his features were relaxing back into the handsome face she'd loved as a girl. He was grayer and more grizzled and needed the bath desperately but he was still in there. This was how she wanted to see him. Not laid out on the floor of the safe room, helpless and wounded.

"Cyrus," she sighed in exasperation. "I *never* forgot you. But that didn't mean that I was free to throw myself into your arms. I have a position here, one I've worked hard for."

His lips twisted into a sarcastic smile even as his eyes fluttered shut. "Sure, because you've always cared for what other people thought. Get dressed, Emily. Leave the soap. I'll wash myself."

"You will do no such thing," she snapped. One constant in her life, no matter if she'd been Emily Franklin, Emily Weatherspoon or Mistress, was that people did not say *no* to her. It simply wasn't done.

"At least put the dress back on," he said in a weary tone that made it clear he knew he'd lost the fight.

She snorted. "And ruin it? I am risking my neck, my livelihood and—" And her heart. Again. But she didn't say that. "And my position in this town to save your sorry hide. If you think I'm going to risk a French silk gown sewn by Worth himself, then you are gravely mistaken."

He opened his mouth to argue but she cut him off. "Men pay good money for a hot bath in this establishment, Cyrus. They pay better money to have a nude woman soap up their bodies for them. The least you could do is enjoy the experience." With that, she stripped off her shift, stepped into the tub, and took the cloth in hand.

She sat on the edge of the tub and lathered up the fine French soap. Honestly, she didn't know what he'd do, but she couldn't say she was surprised when he stayed silent as she began to wash his feet. He tensed at her touch but as she moved the cloth over his skin in deliberate circles, he relaxed. He wasn't filthy, but he smelled of dirt and sweat and blood and she had smelled that on him enough.

His legs were still powerfully made. The years had been kind to him, she thought as she glanced up at his chest. Gunshot wounds notwithstanding. He wasn't the same muscled young man of his youth. He'd gotten broader in both the chest and the waist. His chest still had some definition to it and she had the irrational urge to spread her hands across his chest and see if he felt as good as he looked. Because she knew men hid a great many sins behind their waistcoats and jackets. A man who looked powerful and muscled when dressed could be revealed to be a scrawny sapling with a good deal of padding and a great tailor. She'd lain with men who had guts that resulted from too much beer and whiskey, men who had bigger breasts than she did, men who had members that were little more than her pinkie finger.

Cyrus was none of those things. Even in his unaroused state, he'd still been the perfect size, matched to his body. Any good whore, and Emily was the best, knew that men who were well-endowed were more trouble than they were worth, but men with small members required too much careful platitudes and just the right amount of play-acting.

She hadn't made his knees when he spoke. "How many?"

For the barest second, she considered pretending she didn't know what he was talking about. But this was *Cyrus*. "Who keeps count?"

He snorted. "Never figured you for a lady of the night, Emily."

She grinned. "Cyrus, please. I am a whore. Call a spade a spade. And besides," she went on rather more quickly than she'd planned because suddenly she didn't want to hear that word come out of his mouth. "I kissed you when I was fourteen. You cannot tell me you didn't realize I was a wanton even then."

Her first kiss. No, she didn't keep count. How could she? She only remembered the important moments in her life. Selling the plantation. Her wedding and the subsequent disappointing elimination of her virtue. The death of her husband. Madame Collette in Omaha City, who'd saved her life.

Her first kiss.

With him.

She knelt in the water, straddling his knees so she could wash his upper legs. He didn't protest nor did he make a move for her. This was rather like what had come before that first kiss, a comfortable familiarity with each other's person. He trusted her to wash him, just as she had trusted him to hold her.

"That's a lie, Emily." His eyes had drifted shut as she scrubbed the sweat and dirt off him. "You weren't a wanton then. Curious and rebellious, but not wanton." She looked up and he cracked one eye at her. "Wantons don't marry preacher men."

She smiled. God, she'd missed this man. What

she'd had with Cyrus had never been just lust—or even just attraction. He'd never bowed to her, no matter the difference in their stations. He'd always just been someone she could talk to.

When was the last time she'd just talked to someone else?

"You ever hear from Junie and Liza?"

The question stopped her hand on his thigh. Not even Samuel and Della knew about her sisters. It felt so good to hear their names spoken out loud, to know that her sisters were real people. Because there were days when it felt like she'd dreamed them up. "I hire a Pinkerton agent once a year and put notices in papers. I haven't given up on them."

His hand covered hers. She stared at that touch for a moment and then lifted her gaze to his. Suddenly, her throat tightened because Cyrus understood. "They haven't given up on you, either."

She blinked, willing her eyes not to tear up. "You think?"

"I know." He squeezed her fingers.

Emily did not cry. She simply didn't. "They may not care for me if I find them, you know. They were such good girls." And she wasn't. She hadn't been one for a long time.

She pulled her fingers free of his and went back to washing him. As she got closer to his cock, she could see him hardening. She went to stroke the soapy cloth over his length when he grabbed her hand again. "Don't."

She scowled at him. "I can take care of you, Cyrus."

He closed his eyes and, after a brief pause, gave his head the tiniest of shakes. "No."

That pause told her things—like the fact that he wanted her and was trying to restrain himself.

Well, to hell with that. "Why not? I don't have regrets, you know. Regrets are an emotional indulgence that I don't have time for. I don't regret selling the plantation. I have never regretting splitting the money up amongst the freedmen and women. And," she added when he opened his eyes and his mouth to ask. "I don't regret marrying Phineas or becoming a whore. In fact, of all the things I've done, I only have one regret. *One.*"

"I have trouble believing there's only one thing you regret."

"You," she said softly, scooting up further so that his erection was nestled against the lips of her pussy. "I regret that you and I only ever had that single kiss. And now that you're here, I'm not going to regret you any more."

She wasn't sure what she expected Cyrus to do when she straddled him. Men of her acquaintance generally reacted the same way—with animal lust that they knew they no longer had to restrain for the sake of propriety.

Even though she was no longer a rose in the first bloom, her reputation as a lover without compare had, until recently, had men fumbling out of their trousers as fast as they could.

So she expected Cyrus to be at least excited. Pleased that they were finally going to consummate their relationship, decades after they'd begun their courtship.

"Emily, *no*," he said, gripping her around the hips and holding her steady.

At least he had the decency to sound sad about it, she thought in frustration. "Why not, Cyrus? I want you and you can't tell me you don't want me, too," she added, pointedly shifting against his growing erection. She was wet for him already.

She'd missed sex. But more than that, she'd missed him.

He sighed, a movement that had their bodies touching again. She fought the urge to grind against him. He leaned his head back and closed his eyes. "Sweetheart, I was *shot*. I couldn't even walk down the stairs under my own power. I'm not going to do myself proud with you and if this happens, I'm not going to leave you disappointed."

"I don't like that *if*," she said quietly. "This isn't about me taking my pleasure of you. This is about me taking care of you." She leaned into him, her nipples stiffening as they brushed his chest. Heat blossomed where their skin touched, a fire waiting to catch and burn. "Let me take care of you, Cyrus. I at least owe you this much."

After seeing those scars on his back... she owed him so much more. But there was little she could do about it now. When she had him safely away from the Jeweled Ladies and Brimstone then could she solve the problem that was Cyrus Franklin.

He continued to hold her still atop of him and a new thought occurred to her. Cyrus was the most honorable, noble man she'd ever known and she'd known so many. He wouldn't allow himself to take her if...

A shiver ran over her skin. "Are you married?" She'd never had a problem sleeping with married men.

69

They were some of her best customers. But if he was, Cyrus wouldn't break his vows and she would never have him. Never. She was being ridiculous about this. She had absolutely no right to feel possessive of Cyrus.

"Never was," he said. He hadn't let go of her hips, hadn't pushed her off. "Lived with a woman for a while in Atlanta, but we went our separate ways. She wanted more than I could give and she got a better offer."

And still he held her. Emily took that as a positive sign and began to wash his chest. "That's good," she decided. "I didn't like to think of you alone all these years."

"Did you like to think of me at all?" The question came out as little more than a whisper.

"All the time," she admitted.

His fingers dug into her hips. "Then why, Emily? Why have we lived like strangers—enemies—for the last seven years? Why did you lock me out of your life? Why..." he took a deep breath and opened his eyes. "Why did you save me?"

Chapter Six

It was hard to think. Dangerous, even. All Cyrus could focus on was *not* thrusting against Emily, on not taking what she so generously offered. The strain of holding himself back was making him shake. It would be easier if he were in this tub with Mistress. But he wasn't. He didn't know how he could tell the difference, just that he could.

After seven years of watching and waiting and worrying about her, she had finally come for him. And that was the only thought—well, that and the hole in his shoulder—that kept him from taking her.

She sighed so heavily that little waves spread out from where her body was submerged in the water and lapped against his skin. If he died now, he would go a happy man because she felt so right atop of him. Her flesh felt right under his fingertips. It was finally right that there was nothing between them.

"I suppose..." Another deep sigh. "I was afraid, Cyrus. I have not been Emily for so long that until I saw you on the street, I had almost convinced myself that she didn't exist anymore. I'm a very powerful woman, you know. And the Emily you knew was not. She could not protect her sisters and she could not protect you." As she said this, her hands drifted up his chest to his shoulders and then, leaning her weight against him, she dipped her fingers down his back.

He stiffened. She didn't—*hell*. She had seen the scars. He'd been unconscious for a day or two. She'd checked his wound, no doubt. Damn it all to hell.

"Yes," she said in a gentle tone that he didn't like. "I'm not the only one who's been hiding things, am I?"

"Don't change the subject," he got out through gritted teeth.

God, the weight of her breasts against his chest… it would be so easy just to slide into her and let oblivion wipe away the pain, the years. He'd had all of four lovers in his lifetime and none since he'd spotted her walking along the street of Brimstone, like a dream come to life. He may have hidden the scars from her, but he hadn't lied about not wanting to disappoint her.

She leaned back, leaving his chest cold. When nothing happened after a moment, he opened his eyes. No, this was the girl he'd known. But the girl he'd known hadn't had this body, those breasts. The things he wanted to do with those breasts… He closed his eyes again.

When she touched him next, he jumped, but it was only the washcloth on one of his arms. She peeled his hand away from her waist and scrubbed every inch of him with what he hoped was tender care.

"Fine. I won't change the subject but we are coming back to those scars, sir. My father is not worth protecting. He never was."

He almost laughed at that. How could she think that he would protect Chester Franklin? The man was evil incarnate. And the sad thing was, he probably wasn't the worst master out there. Cyrus had heard rumors—they all had. Chester Franklin was evil in a very everyday sort of way. He raped his slaves and beat them for minor transgressions. There was nothing exceptional about him, except for his daughter. God only knew how Franklin had produced Emily.

"Wasn't protecting him. But he's dead and you're not and neither am I, so you first. Were you afraid that I'd tell everyone who you really are?" That was the only thing that had ever made sense to him and even then, it didn't. Her only living family was some uncle who had disowned her when she had sold the plantation and married Phineas Weatherspoon. Well, that and her half-sisters and there was no way they could find her when she was living under an assumed name. Hell, Mistress wasn't even a name at all. It was barely a title of respect. All it did was guarantee that Junie and Liza would never find her. And, for the life of him, he couldn't figure out why anyone in this three-horse town would care that she'd been Emily Weatherspoon. Still, it hadn't been his place to name her and she had made it quite clear that he had no place with her.

"Mistress has no past and no future," Emily sighed. "She is a creation of the present. Every night, like a phoenix, she rises anew for one purpose and one purpose only—to make men feel powerful and relieve them of their coin."

"That's two things."

She ignored him, moving onto his other arm. He settled the clean hand back against her skin. But he didn't dare open his eyes and he didn't interrupt her.

"That's the secret, you know. Not having a

73

history. Men can fantasize about whatever they want you to be. I'm a blank slate to every single person in this town except you, Cyrus. You could undo it all. You still can." She said this last bit in such a small voice. He was so tempted to believe she was telling tales, trying to find something, anything to excuse her poor behavior. Except for that last bit. There was truth in there. Her behavior was still poor toward him. But maybe what she was saying was true, too.

"Why would anyone here believe me? I'm just a nobody."

"That is so patently not the truth, Cyrus, and you know it." He couldn't help but grin at her sharp tone. "You are... a mirror. We both are. It's just that I reflect back to the people of this town what they want the fine silks, the jewels, the freedom to do as they wish—and you, by taking in the poor and the broken, the weak and the needy, you show them what they really are. All the good Christians of Brimstone want to do away with me, and yes, there are many who would love to see me burn. They care more about what people do behind closed doors than they do about helping the downtrodden. Christianity for them isn't about the love of a just God, it's about judgment."

He considered that. "You are a sinner, though."

She laughed, a light sound that filled him with happiness. It was a memory brought back to life, that laugh. "I have never claimed to be anything else. I don't follow the rules they make themselves follow and they hate me for choosing freedom. Now you... you're a different story. The opposite side of the coin. They don't like you not because you're black and not because you are a former slave, but because you show them how poor their version of Christianity really is. That's why they hate you. The fact that you are black only allows them to hide their hatred behind something familiar. How dare you show them up, Cyrus?"

He looked at her, trying to store everything about this moment in his memory, just like the time he'd kissed her was permanently etched in his mind. "I've always dared, I seem to recall."

"You've dared to be daring," she agreed, grinning broadly at him. If they were still children, tucked back along the creek where they'd hidden under the bank that had eroded away over time, he'd shove her into the water for her cheekiness. But he could do no such thing. Only one of his arms worked at the moment and he couldn't be entirely sure it'd ever function properly again. Besides, if he moved, he wouldn't shove her. Kiss her, maybe. Ravish her, most likely. But not shove her.

"It is not the same for me, but it is, in a way," she went on. "I am above my station in life as a woman with more power and freedom than anyone else in this town. I represent the manifestation of all of their unnatural urges and they see those urges walk freely about this town while they themselves feel shame at wanting. Oh, how they hate me. Even the ones who'll stroll in tonight, ready to spend their money chasing their private shames. They hate that they must entrust me with their deepest secret desires. And secrets have power."

He stared at her. It made sense, in a perverse sort of way. "You're not the only brothel in this town."

Her grin was sly and knowing, sending a shiver

75

down his back because this was Mistress and even nude, washing a wounded man, she was a woman who got what she wanted. Even him.

"Ah, but I'm the one to be reckoned with. I own part of the other brothels, to keep them clean and make sure they treat their girls well. With very few exceptions, I know *everything* about everyone in this town." The look of raw power faded and Emily was back, looking tired. "They want to get rid of me to keep their secrets safe and they want to get rid of you so you will not demonstrate how much their morals have failed. But they dress up their hatred under the guise of propriety. If they put us together, Cyrus, we might both be dead within the week. For your own safety, I kept my distance from you. For my safety as well," she added quickly when he frowned at her. "I am not so selfless as all that. I keep my good deeds hidden and you..." She leaned forward and stroked his cheek. "You have always been my best deed."

It was a lot of good talk, all of it. "I thought you hated me. You wouldn't talk to me, wouldn't look at me. How could I think anything but that you hated me?"

"Never," she whispered. She finished his other hand and it naturally settled back around her waist. It was as if they had always been like this, some twenty-five odd years notwithstanding. "I thought... I was afraid," she corrected, "you would look at me and see what I have become and want nothing more to do with me. I was afraid that you had become a different person as well. So much has changed, Cyrus, and it was foolish of me, but I wanted to keep my perfect memories of you and me just that."

There hadn't been anything perfect about it and

they both knew it. He had been enslaved and every conversation with her, every touch, had been him putting his life on the line. That kiss had nearly killed him.

"It was enough for me," she went on, "to know you were alive and well. It was enough to know that I could help keep you that way without risking both of our lives."

He shot her a look. "What do you mean?"

She sat back, a stern look on her face at complete odds with her nudity. "You don't believe Sheriff Cutler let you go last time out of the kindness of his heart, do you? Honestly, Cyrus. He's an honorable enough man, but it took three hundred damned dollars so he'd release you before the posse came. Luckily for you," she went on as his mouth dropped open, "I have done that with enough regularity over the years that it did not draw any special comment from him. I don't think he enjoys seeing people of color lynched, but he's just one man. It takes money and that's what I have. Then most of the people he lets go, they show up at your house, don't they? Black men, mostly, scared out of their minds, sure that they weren't going to live to see the morning? Confused as to why the white sheriff kicked them out and told them start running while they still could?"

He blinked, then blinked again. She was right. Once, maybe twice a year, a man would come running, begging to be hid from the posse that they were sure was fast on their heels with a noose and a gun. None of them were sure why they'd been spared.

She did hide her good deeds, didn't she? "You did that?"

"Emily Weatherspoon did that. Emily Franklin did that. Mistress kept a man of the law in her good graces with her money. In fact, making sure that the sheriff has had an irregular, but impressive bonus added to his salary every so often is probably the reason he didn't search this place looking for your sorry hide and it's probably the reason he hasn't been back in three days. But if we had a known connection, Cyrus, I wouldn't have been able to keep him out. And that, more than my feelings for you and more than your feelings that you may or may not have for me, is the reason that I have not come to you before now."

She stood then and he couldn't help but watch as the water sheeted off her body. Emily Franklin had been a slip of a girl on the cusp of womanhood. Emily Weatherspoon had been a righteous young bride hell-bent on spreading the good word of the Lord. But Mistress? She had broad hips and luscious thighs that he was desperate to feel clamped around his waist. Her stomach was rounded but her waist was narrow. He could still see the imprint the corset left on her skin. And her breasts, even in his dreams he had not imagined a pair of breasts so lush and full as hers. But some things hadn't changed. Her skin was still creamy white and her eyes still flashed with that righteous indignation. She was temptation embodied and God help him, he was tempted.

The last time he'd succumbed to the temptation...

"Lean forward," she ordered. "I'm going to wash your back and you're going to tell me why you lied to me about that whipping."

"Ancient history, Emily." But she'd already seen the scars. There was no point in hiding, so he leaned forward.

"As I recall, I got word that you had been whipped for stepping out of line with the Master's daughter and by the time I could sneak away, two or three days had passed." She applied the washcloth to his back and scrubbed hard. "As I recall, I found you sitting on your pallet in your home—"

"Shack," he corrected.

"Shack," she agreed, "with a clean shirt on your body and your back firmly pressed against the wall. As I recall," she repeated again with more fervor, "you assured me you'd only got five lashes, that he hadn't swung the whip hard at all and everything was fine. Just *fine*."

He felt her fingers moving over the scars. Counting, he realized.

"That is generally what I recall as well." It had been one of the hardest things he'd done—outside of not screaming during the beating. He'd kept his back and the bloody shirt pressed firmly against the wall where Emily wouldn't be able to see and he had lied through his teeth to her. It had hurt almost as much as the beating itself.

"Why are you protecting that man?"

"How could you think I would protect him?" he scoffed. "I was protecting you."

"There's more than forty scars here, not counting your brand-new addition." Her voice was brittle. "They all run together. I can't tell where they stop and start. That is a far cry from five, Cyrus."

He rested his head on his knees as she scrubbed. There was something hypnotic about those circles she was rubbing into his back. If he didn't want her so much, he would be tempted to go back to sleep to savor every moment of this strange bath. "Fifty. Fifty lashes was the price for kissing you." When she gasped, he looked up and added, "It was worth it, though."

Her hand fluttered to her chest as an honest-to-God blush pinked her cheeks and there she was, the girl he'd fallen in love with all those years ago.

"Do you realize that that may be the most romantic thing anyone has ever said to me?"

"Not a lot of romance in your line of work?" he asked, resting his head back on his knees.

"Not for me. I do create a certain amount of romance, but it is for the benefit of the gentlemen callers."

"That preacher you married? Not big on romance, hmm?"

She laughed at that. "Phineas? Heavens, no. Such a good man, but not what one would call a romantic. He was far too pious to allow himself to enjoy bed sports."

That brought up his next big question. He'd long since figured that Emily had been in Brimstone for several years before he'd arrived, stumbling upon her completely by accident. But no one in town knew where she'd come from. What had happened between the day he'd watched her and her preacher head out in a wagon and her arrival in Brimstone was a complete mystery. "What happened to him?"

"Oh, that. We wound up in Indian country, trying to 'convert the heathens' as he liked to say. I was in charge of the schoolroom, since I had experience teaching people to read. I wasn't entirely sure that they needed to accept Christ into their hearts—at least not with the zeal that he did. They had their ways and who was I to tell them that they were wrong?"

He smiled, even though she couldn't see it. That was the most Emily-like thing she'd said today.

"But I knew that they would need to know how to read and write if they were going to survive their encounters with white people. You can lean back down."

He did so. The water was cooling but it was still quite warm. He felt so clean, it was almost as if he had been reborn. Maybe he had been. Even if his house was still standing, he wasn't sure he could go back to being Free Cyrus Franklin, scourge of Brimstone and opponent of Mistress of the Jeweled Ladies. "I take it that some people objected to his sermons?"

"Sickness spread through the Pawnee tribe and they blamed him for it. I suspect some of them blamed me, as well, but…"

"But you'd made friends." Emily could make anyone like her. Men that should have wanted to break her neck for what her father's overseers did instead protected Emily because she snuck them food and supplies and taught their children how to read and gave them hope that one day, they could be something more than chattel.

"To a degree."

He opened his eyes and saw that she was sitting on the edge of the tub again. He wanted her to come back down so that they could be skin to skin, but he was exhausted and no matter how much she wanted to take care of him, he would *not* disappoint her.

"I was also exotic to them and that made me valuable. I saw my choices quite clearly. I could defend my maidenly virtue and be killed relatively quickly or I could give their leader what he wanted and survive." She crossed her arms around her waist, curling slightly into a small ball. "I chose to survive." She lifted her head and smiled a smile that did not reach her eyes. "Besides, I had always had that wanton streak in me. By the time I made it back to a white town, about seven months later?" She shrugged, as if being held by a tribe in sexual bondage for months on end was nothing to concern herself with. "By then, I had received quite an education in what men wanted from women and how women could give it to them. The madam in Omaha City took me in and taught me everything else I needed to know. Cheap whores were exactly that—cheap, but Madame Collette was French and she created this brothel that was not merely soiled doves fluttering around a saloon. It was glamorous and the women were beautiful and talented and she promised that I could have control of my life back and do the good deeds that had nearly gotten me killed. Men would pay good money for the illusion of the lady, after all. So that's what I became all over again."

She recited these facts as if she were telling a boring story instead of relating the murder of her husband and her descent from preacher's wife to prostitute.

"Emily."

She looked up at him and he held out his hand. For the barest second, he thought she wouldn't take it, but then she did.

"I'm glad you chose to survive."

The shadows dissipated from around her eyes. After all, the things she had been discussing were all ancient history.

"I'm glad you survived, too."

"I would've gone with you, you know." After she had given him his freedom, he had all but begged her to take him with her. The fact that she hadn't—well, it'd been the first time he had wondered maybe he didn't mean as much to her as she meant to him. It hadn't been the last.

"I know. But to what end, Cyrus? So that you could have died by Phineas's side? Or been killed when you tried to defend my tattered honor? No." She stood, pulling her hand away from his. Moving carefully, she stepped out of the tub and folded a large towel around her body. "Because that's what would've happened." She looked down at him and the force of the longing in her gaze was so powerful that, if he hadn't been sitting already, he would've been knocked on his behind. "You may not believe this, but I love you. I have always loved you and I will always love you."

It shouldn't have meant anything to him. They were just words and she had no doubt uttered them countless times to countless other people. His heart leapt anyway because finally, *finally*, it was an acknowledgment of the truth that had existed between them from the very beginning. "I would do anything for you, Emily. That hasn't changed either."

The corners of her mouth pulled down as her eyes got wet. "Good," she said softly. "Then when I send you away, you'll go?"

"Send me *away*?" His voice echoed off the metal tub and the tiled walls. "What are you talking about?"

She didn't come closer, didn't reassure him with a simple touch. She kept her distance and it was almost as if he could see her putting on the armor that was Mistress. "Cyrus, if there is one thing I know to be true about you and I, it's that it is dangerous for us to be together. I've made arrangements," she went on before he could protest. "I have to get you out of this house and then I have to get you out of Brimstone. Someone set you up and we can't possibly have much time before they come looking for you again. I *will* do everything within my power to keep you safe. That's all I need. To know that you're safe."

And with that, she scooped up her shift and her corset and strode from the bathing room, leaving Cyrus to wonder if he meant anything to her at all.

Chapter Seven

She was not crying. Crying was a useless emotion and did not solve problems.

Right now, the problem was in her bathtub. Naked and hard for her and so damned honorable that he wouldn't let her give him the gift of release. The gift of consummation.

She dried her body briskly and was slipping her shift over her head when she heard the sound of water splashing in the bathroom. Oh, Lord. He wasn't going to—

But he was. He already had. By the time she made it to the doorway, Cyrus was out of the tub. His brow wrinkled with concentration and he was breathing heavily, his good arm held out from his side as if he was walking on a railroad tie and needed the balance. Slowly, he lowered his hand and opened his eyes.

The look he gave her could have flattened her, he was so angry. "You're going to send me away?" he asked in a dangerously calm voice.

She had not often seen him mad. She knew he possessed the capacity for rage. He'd hated being enslaved, hated seeing his mother and his siblings sold away as punishment for befriending the master's daughter. She had raged at her father on his behalf because she knew that he wasn't able to.

"It's for the best," she said, but her voice shook.

"You just offered to have sex with me because I was your regret. Your one regret! His voice rose into a shout, pushing her back. He took an unsteady step toward her.

"Cyrus—you're wounded! Be careful!"

He advanced on her. She wasn't afraid, but she suddenly realized that she still didn't know the man he was now. "I won't go, Emily. I'm no longer yours to order around. You don't get to decide my fate."

The back of her knees hit the bed and she sat with a hard thump. Cyrus loomed over her, his eyes dark and his hands clenched into fists by his side. A little thrill of pleasure went through her. She should have been scared, but she wasn't. No matter what the years had wrought between them, she knew this man would never hurt her.

When they had been children, though Cyrus had never seemed a child to her, he had been careful not to touch her. She'd been the master's daughter and he a slave. That was how it was supposed to have been, although it had never been the reality. As he had grown from a boy into a man, she had been the one to break the invisible barriers between them. A hand on his arm, then on his shoulder.

She'd been the one to sit so close to him that their bodies touched from hip to shoulder as they hid in the little carved out burrow. The only time he had ever touched her first had been the day of the kiss, when he had found her crying her eyes out because she had lost her sisters. And even then, all he had done was put his arm around her shoulders and hold her. She had been the one to kiss him.

He was the one who paid the price for it.

"All right," she said, leaning back on her elbows and staring up at him. Oh, if things had been different, if he'd been born a free man and she'd been born anyone other than Chester Franklin's daughter...

His arms were shaking and she couldn't tell if that was because of strain from his injury or because he was holding himself back. God, she was tired of him holding back. She was tired of pretending that she didn't need him in her life. How many nights had she lain awake in this very bed, staring at the ceiling and wondering if he hated her for how she treated him?

How many times, over decades of debauchery and sin, had his face assembled itself in her mind's eye as she went through the motions of intimacy with someone else?

How many nights—actually, early mornings—in the last seven years had she slid on men's clothes and made it as far as the livery stables, finally deciding to ride out and see him? Not as Mistress, but as Emily. Finally, again, she could be Emily, but only with him.

But even pretending she was making love with Cyrus instead of fucking some nameless, faceless customer or plunging the wooden cock into her own body wasn't the same as this—him standing over her, his cock hard and pointed at her as if it were a compass and she were true north, his eyes dark with want.

If it were anyone else standing before her, she'd lean forward and suck his cock into her mouth. She'd use her hands and her tongue and her teeth to give him a few moments of excruciating pleasure before he came. Just long enough that no one would feel cheated out of his coin, but short enough that she would have plenty of time for the next customer. But she'd already offered and he'd refused. She didn't know where that left them now.

"All right," she repeated again, giving him permission. "What *do* you want, Cyrus?"

"You're not sending me away." There was no question, but a statement of fact. Cyrus vibrated with the power of it and Emily's sex began to dampen. It had been a long time, after all. "You hear me, Emily? I won't go. Because you're not the only one with regrets. I regret that I took your money and walked away instead of following you and that fool husband of yours. I regret I didn't keep you safe. I regret that I didn't look for you once I realized I was never going to forget you. I regret that, when I found you—completely by accident—I once again let you dictate the terms of our relationship. Because you make terrible decisions, Emily. You may run this town and you may run this brothel, but you don't run me. Not anymore."

With that, he fell to his knees. It was such an ungainly gesture than Emily cried out an alarm. Had he fallen?

No. Using only his left hand, he awkwardly jerked at the hem of her chemise, pushing it up over her bare thighs. "I won't disappoint you," he said, his voice strained as she spread her legs for him. "But I'm done waiting on you, Emily."

He pressed a kiss against the top of her thigh, then another over the hair of her mound. Moving with deliberation, he used his good hand to spread her pussy lips and then he kissed her there, too, right on her little pearl of pleasure.

This was different—all of it. Heat built from the inside and she ran her tongue over her lips. There were men who liked to lick a pussy while they jerked off, but even that most intimate of acts was about their pleasure. Any pussy would do. No one had ever licked her pussy because they wanted to give *her* pleasure. Not even her husband, may his soul rest in peace. Sexual congress was about reproduction for that man. Never about joy. And, sinner that she was, she was going to enjoy Cyrus. She wanted to learn everything about him, his likes and dislikes. She had a few guesses—there would be no sadism or bondage in this bed. But more than just the act, she wanted...

His tongue swept over her in a move that was almost lazy. He wouldn't rush, not her Cyrus. He'd savor every single moment of their time together.

This was what she didn't get from her wooden phallus—this care, this love. She had to shove her fist into her mouth to keep from crying out as his tongue stroked over her sex again. He made a noise high in the back of his throat and then he set his lips back to her pearl, pulling the tender flesh into his mouth with his teeth and sucking. Her hips bucked and this time, she did cry out.

"That's it, sweetheart," he murmured against her flesh. "Oh, Em."

She wanted to stay with him. It was a selfish, weak emotion because no matter what he said or did in a fit of passion, it wasn't safe for them to be together. But she wanted to welcome him into her body, and then, when they'd sated their lust, she wanted to stay in bed with him and sleep in his arms. That was exactly where she wanted to wake up, too.

God, she wanted so much.

She shook the sorrow away and refocused her attention on the present. Experimentally, she stroked her hand over his wiry hair. He leaned into her touch but he didn't pull his good arm away from her bare thighs.

"I never controlled you, you know," she told him as he looked up at her, his head still buried between her legs. "If I had, I would've had you between my thighs before I was sixteen. I would've had you for two years, maybe even longer. I would've spent the long afternoons fucking you until we were too tired to move." He groaned and licked her harder. Did he like naughty talk in bed, then? "I would've slipped out of the house to sleep in your arms at night and awoken you in the morning with my mouth everywhere on you."

Because that was the truth. She would've given him everything and taken what he could give. But it would have been wrong. Maybe she'd known then. Every touch between them would've been a threat on his life. Even if he hadn't lied to her about the number of lashes he'd gotten for a simple kiss, she still knew that being with him could have been the death of him. She could've taken whatever she wanted from him and at worst, gotten pregnant. Her father would've gotten rid of the baby and married her off to someone who wouldn't care that she spoiled herself. She would've been miserable and unhappy, but alive. And if there was one thing she knew about herself, it was that she would have survived. Cyrus, however, wouldn't have lived to see the next dawn. Or, if he had, he would have prayed for the mercy of death.

They had not been equals. So, as much as she had always regretted having nothing more than a kiss, she'd known it was best. If she'd taken her pleasure of him then, they might not be here together now.

"I've dreamed of being between your thighs," he murmured, his voice reverential. With his left hand, he spread her wet pussy even wider. "I wondered how you'd look, taste."

She shifted her hips toward him, the smell of sex tingeing the air with its sweet perfume. "I want you inside of me," she said, her voice a needy whisper. "You won't disappoint me, Cyrus and I'll make damn sure you're not disappointed, either."

He stared up at her with something that looked like fear. Was he afraid he couldn't perform? He was hard. She could do the rest. And, she realized, she would have to. Cyrus's right arm hung limp and beads of perspiration broke out on his forehead. Damn it all, she wanted him so much she could barely think straight. She couldn't let him kneel on the floor and do all the work.

"Wait."

The groan of pain issued forth from his chest. "*Wait*, sweetheart? Haven't I waited long enough?"

"On the bed. Please," she added, lest he think she was trying to boss him around again. "Because I am going to have you and you are going to have me and I can't leave you on the floor. Unless, after we're done and you're too wrung out to move, you want to explain to Ruby how you got there in the first place?"

He snorted in what she hoped was amusement, but he sat back on his heels, his fingertips tracing down her leg. "Fine. Where do you want me?"

Moving gently, she got under his left side and helped him back to his feet. He swayed as he stood. Once he was steady, she said, "One second."

She moved quickly, turning down the bed and arranging the pillows so that his head would be raised to the best angle. She laid a towel over the pillows so, if his wound seeped, it would not ruin the Belgian lace. Then she carefully guided him onto the bed, swinging his legs around and making sure the pillows supported him. He didn't argue with her. Smart man.

"Now what?" he asked when she had settled him in. Although his face had been tight, the lines on his forehead relaxed and she knew that she'd made the right call.

"You tell me. Do you need a rest?" It would nigh onto kill her to pull the blankets up to his chin and leave him be, but that was his choice. She would not push him.

He held out his hand for her. "I will when we're done. Let me put my mouth on you, sweetheart."

How many times had she drawn off her she chemise and watched the man's eyes gleam with appreciation? How many times had she put an extra sway into her hips and watched the man's cock twitch in anticipation? None of this was new to her. But at the same time, it was. Desire crashed over her with a force that surprised her. Excitement tightened her nipples and flooded her pussy with wetness. She was already more aroused simply stripping for Cyrus than she had been for any man in years. Decades, even. Years since

92

the sexual act had done anything for her except make her that much richer.

Oh, she'd forgotten this. She had forgotten a need so strong it made her knees weak. She had forgotten the power she felt when a man looked at her with naked longing and she had forgotten the power she gave up when she submitted to that longing.

She moaned and cupped her breasts, stroking over her nipples. They were two hard pebbles against her skin, tight under her fingertips. "Where will you put your mouth? Here?"

Cyrus groaned. "Yeah. Let me suckle you. You like it hard or easy?"

Her breath caught in her throat to hear such things from his mouth. This was no longer the cautious boy, but a man who knew the pleasures of the flesh. A man who could meet her as an equal.

God, she loved him.

But she didn't rush to him. Not yet. What were a few more moments when it'd already been this long? "Hard, Cyrus. I want you *hard* here. And here," she added, stroking her hands over her stomach and down over the cleft between her legs. "Did you like putting your mouth against my pussy and tasting my cream, Cyrus?"

"Babe," he all but whimpered, his hips shifting on the bed, his erection huge with wanting. "Please."

This was more familiar to her, a man begging with need, pleasure promised for all. This wouldn't be the only time. She'd make sure of it. "I can't wait, my darling. We'll have time to do it slow but I need you inside of me right now." She slipped onto the bed and straddled him. Instantly, his hard cock was rubbing along the folds of her pussy, getting wet with her juices.

93

"That a promise, Emily?" His good hand gripped her hip and he stilled. "Because I won't go. Don't make me go."

She hitched her body up, but before she could grab hold of his staff and guide him into her body, his cock sprang up on its own and his tip found her opening. True north, indeed.

If it were anyone else, she'd lie. She'd spout the easy platitudes of false love and even falser pledges of loyalty because that's what the gentlemen callers paid for—the pretense of love and duty and the sexual freedom to do whatever they wanted that came with it. But she couldn't lie to Cyrus. "I'll do my best," she said, lowering herself onto him. "Oh, Cyrus," she moaned as her body opened for his.

This was what she'd been missing—the way hard flesh thrust up to penetrate her softness, but yet, at the same time, the hardness of his cock had a give to it. Cyrus's cock wasn't a bruising foreign object. It was a part of her that belonged, as much as the air she breathed or the wine she drank.

"Don't make me leave, babe," he said, lifting his head and staring her in the eye. "I couldn't bear it to lose you again."

She paused only long enough to shove another pillow behind his head for support and then she began to ride him in earnest.

And it was a gift. That's all she could think as she rose up and slammed her hips down onto his, over and over. He pulled her down so that he could suckle her tit into his mouth, pulling on the nipple and skimming his teeth over the hardened flesh.

She knew how to find her own pleasure in sex, of

course. But for so many years, this act had been… a performance. Instead of losing herself to the joining of flesh, she always had been gauging the reaction of her client, adjusting her actions to better satisfy him or her or them. She'd rarely lost herself to the slap of skin against skin, the thrust of hard against soft, the pull of tongue and teeth.

She threw back her head and slid her fingers between where their bodies were joined, stroking her pearl as she took him inside her, again and again. *Home*, she thought through the haze of wanton—yes, wanton—lust. She'd finally come home.

She worked her hand back so that her fingertips could stroke over his shaft with every thrust while the palm of her hand ground against her pearl.

"Emily," he moaned against her tit before sucking the other nipple so hard that bright bursts of pain flashed over her before he soothed them away with his tongue.

The sensations rocketed through her, her body clenching around his. She buried her free hand in his hair, holding him to her. Up, down—he filled her again and again, a balm for her soul.

It was coming, her climax. She could feel the wave of it cresting, bigger and stronger than anything she'd felt in ages.

"God, Cyrus," she hissed and, clever man that he was, he heard the need in her voice. His mouth clamped down on her nipple again, setting off another round of bright sparks of pain that burned into pleasure. With his good hand, he gripped her ass, digging his fingers into her flesh and doing his damnedest to thrust in harder and harder.

Emily surrendered to it, to him. She let that wave crest, keening as her body broke and broke again. Cyrus made a guttural noise in the back of his throat and then threw his head back, the cords of his neck straining as he came deep inside of her.

For a taut moment, they were frozen in their poses as the orgasms robbed them of everything—movement, speech—everything but pleasure.

Then everything about Emily went soft and she fell, boneless, onto his chest, panting heavily. "My," she murmured, somehow managing to push herself up onto her elbows. She didn't want to strain his wound—any more than she already had, that was. "That's what I've been dreaming of for years, Cyrus."

Although his eyes were closed, he managed a smile. "Not a disappointment, I hope?"

"Better than I ever dreamed. I can't wait until you're back at full strength, my darling. I insist you tell me everything you've ever wanted to do and I'll show you everything I know." She drew lazy circles on his chest and then pressed her lips to the same spot before she slid off him.

"Not leaving you," he murmured and she could tell he was already slipping off, the afternoon having finally exhausted him.

It had been selfish of her, no doubt, to tax his energy while he was still injured, but she couldn't regret it. Finally, they'd consummated their relationship. "I know," she said, feeling her throat tighten. "I'll get you cleaned up and you can sleep."

She wet a cloth and wiped away the traces of their lovemaking and made sure to slather on the salve Ruby had left for his injury. Then she pulled the covers up to his chin. His lips twitched into something that might have been a smile when she leaned down and said, "Rest, darling. I'll be back later." Because she loved him and he loved her and God knew they could be great together. She could spend the rest of her life loving him and die a contented woman.

But none of that changed the reality outside of this room. She was still Mistress and she had to protect her position and every woman—and girl—who lived in this house. He was still Free Cyrus Franklin and someone wanted him dead. And if anyone put the two of them together, it would potentially be the end of both of them.

He wouldn't leave her.

But clearly, he couldn't stay.

Chapter Eight

Cyrus woke up on and off all afternoon. The first time, there was a tray with coffee and beef tea on the table beside the bed, along with slices of bread and ham. Cyrus gratefully drank the coffee and broth and made it halfway through the sandwich before he fell back into the most erotic dreams of his life. Emily was everywhere, nude and laughing, her body on his, under his. She'd promised to teach him everything she knew and, at least in his dreams, she knew an awful lot of things.

The next time he woke, hard and aching for her, he could hear music and the sound of laughing emanating throughout the house. For a delirious second, he was going to get dressed and go out and finally see what all the hubbub was about at the Jeweled Ladies. He'd see Emily in her element and maybe that would explain why she'd clung to this life.

He made it as far as the toilet. Indoor plumbing was a gift he'd never enjoyed before, but he managed to figure out the pull handle. However, that little bit of walking was enough to wipe him out.

The room was dark, dusk falling around the town of Brimstone, but not so dark he couldn't see the pitcher of water and another mug of beef tea on the table, along with some cookies and a soft custard so sweet that Cyrus moaned as he ate it. Exhausted, he climbed right back into Emily's huge bed and fell asleep again.

When he startled awake next, it was almost completely dark in the room. Where was he? The sound of a key turning in a lock caught his attention, then the door swung open. Candlelight fell into the room and was quickly snuffed.

Terror dumped into his blood. Was someone here to finish what they'd started in the street? Why didn't he have a gun? "Who's there?"

"It's me, darling," came Emily's soft voice as the door clicked shut and she shot the bolt. "It's three in the morning. Can I get you anything before I turn in?"

The relief was so profound that Cyrus could have cried. Making love to Emily with his tongue and then his body had really happened. "Just come to bed," he said gruffly, almost overwhelmed with emotion. He had the feeling there was something he was supposed to ask about… but his mind was like cotton wool.

She moved quietly around the room without lighting a lamp. He heard the sound of fabric falling, the clink of what sounded like metal against china— her jewelry, maybe?

He'd started to drift off when the mattress sagged and then she was curled up against his side, warm and real and soft and everything he'd ever wanted.

He wasn't so sure he wasn't dreaming, after all.

Cyrus woke with a start. *Isaac.* He was supposed to ask about Isaac. That Jewel, Ruby—she was supposed to ride out last night and see if Isaac and Rob

Boy and Beulah were okay. If Cyrus had been burned out or not.

"Cyrus?" Came the soft voice next to it. The hand stroked over his bare chest. Emily. "It's okay, darling. I'm here. You're fine."

"Isaac?" His throat was dry and it felt like he was trying to see through a fog. He felt like he'd been asleep for four days. Again. "Ruby?"

Emily pushed herself up. Her hair was a tangled mess and her face was creased with sleep. The covers fell off her bare shoulders as she blinked at him. "They're okay."

Something in his chest stilled. "How okay?"

Emily worried at her lower lip with her teeth. "Your friend Isaac got everyone out before…"

The air rushed out of Cyrus's chest just as surely as if someone had punched him. Emily didn't have to say it—his home was gone. It hadn't been much, but it had been his. Hopefully, Isaac had been able to get the money Cyrus had buried out back as well. He had more in a bank in New York City, but it took time to get that cash and he didn't like the idea of being stranded without options.

Emily stared at him, worry creasing her brow. "When Ruby got there, there was nothing but a few smoldering ruins. She was trying to find anything worth saving when your friend appeared out of nowhere and grabbed her. It seems your man Isaac thought that she had come back to finish them off. He doesn't talk much, so we're not sure."

Cyrus closed his eyes. Isaac would never grab a woman like that. He felt like he was missing something. "She okay?"

Emily snorted. "You might not believe it, but Ruby is a lot tougher than she looks. Smarter, too. There are days..."

She looked off in the distance. Some things never changed. Emily lost in thought this morning, sleep still touching her eyes, was exactly the same as she'd been as a girl.

He reached out and stroked his fingers down her bare shoulder to call her back to herself. "Where's Isaac now?"

"The attic. I tell you, that room hasn't seen this much action in years. Your other two guests are up there, as well. Ruby is tending to that poor man. Honestly, she's not sure he'll survive." She tapped her lips with her finger, which caused the sheet to slip lower across her chest. "If he recovers, I'll need to ascertain what their skills are before I decide the best place to send them, of course. I take it that they're married?"

Cyrus nodded. She sounded so briskly efficient, as if one of her whores bringing home three complete strangers and hiding them in the attic was just another day.

She shrugged and brightened. "We'll get it figured out by tonight. I have a guest coming this afternoon—oh, don't give me that look," she admonished when he frowned at her. She followed this up with a gentle smack to his good arm. "It's not like that. I know you may not believe this, Cyrus, but you're the first person to share my bed in over a year. I manage this business. I rarely work anymore."

The cobwebs were beginning to clear from his brain. He must've slept close to sixteen hours.

Experimentally, he tried to rotate his right shoulder. It burned, but it didn't send jagged fingers of pain licking along his body. He was healing.

He mulled over her words as he tried to stretch a little. "So if it's not a client, who's your guest?"

She exhaled, worrying that lower lip again. In another day or so, he'd be able to reach over with his bad arm and pull her toward him so that he could worry that lip for her. It wasn't so bad, being stuck in this beautiful room with indoor plumbing, his meals apparently delivered, sleeping in the biggest, softest bed he'd ever been in and waking up with a nude Emily next to him. If it weren't for the fact that someone was trying to kill him, he might be content to stay here for a long while.

"You have to understand, there are very few people I would trust with a matter this sensitive. There are only four other people who know for certain that you are in this building—Ruby, Samuel, Della and Dolly. Of course some of the other Jewels suspect that you and Dolly are still here, but they know better than to tell tales."

Her gaze sharpened and she looked not just dangerous but murderous and he remembered that she'd shot whoever'd shot him. She could be deadly, his Emily. That was definitely something new. The Emily he'd known way back when might have been prone to fits of righteous indignation, but she never would've hurt another living soul.

"Emily." She always did have a tendency to expound. "Who is your guest?"

"Hank O'Shea." She said with such caution, as if he would burst into a fit of rage at the mention of the mayor's right-hand man. Correction—the former mayor's right-hand man.

Instead, Cyrus burst out laughing. "Why, that's just fine, Emily. I've met Hank before. He's a good man. You think he can help?"

Once again, her face brightened with a warm smile that took ten years off her age. "How did you— oh, never mind," she said, waving the question away. "Mr. O'Shea is perhaps the only person in this town who plays deeper than I do. Or at least, he did. Did you know he figured out I was Emily Weatherspoon?" Her gaze swung up to his face. "Did you tell him that?"

He held his good hand over his chest. "Cross my heart, I never breathed a word of your real name to a single soul."

"I *must* figure out how he found out," she murmured to herself. "But my point is, if there's anyone who can help smuggle you and Dolly out of this house, it's him. With a little luck, he might even be able to figure out who shot you. Unless you have any ideas?" she asked, looking hopeful.

Cyrus shook his head, which blissfully did not make him dizzy. He was definitely on the mend. How much of that was the sleep and how much of that was the sex? "I got an anonymous note. All it said was that you had a girl that you were planning to sell. Isaac didn't see who'd brought it."

She went back to frowning. "Do you know if the Snyders hate you enough to try to kill you?"

"My money's always been good at the dry-goods store."

She scooted closer to him, the sheets falling even

more. Now that he was well rested and the fog of sleep had cleared, he could appreciate the beauty that was Emily Weatherspoon in the morning light. Her nipples were large circles of deep tan with just a hint of rose to them. Last night, he'd had those nipples in his mouth and he made her cry out as he'd sucked on them.

His cock stirred beneath the sheets. He hadn't had sex in seven or eight years before yesterday, but suddenly, he was ready to go all over again.

He shifted his legs, bringing his knees up so that the sheet wouldn't fall over his erection. "What makes you think the Snyders had something to do with it?"

"I sent Samuel to buy dresses for Dolly. They would've been the first people in town to suspect that I had a girl. But," she went on after a moment's pause, "I can't think that they would risk a paying customer—either me or you."

He was inclined to agree. The Snyders ran a thriving business because they catered to the Jewels. However... "Mrs. Snyder does enjoy her gossip, doesn't she?" Something else she'd said niggled at the back of his mind, but he couldn't think straight with her bare breasts on display like that.

"She does. So that narrows down the list of potential people who laid a trap for you to anyone who shopped at the dry-goods store within the last week and a half who Mrs. Snyder likes enough to gossip to." She collapsed back on the bed in defeat. "Cyrus, I don't know how to solve all these problems." Her head popped up. "Don't tell anyone I ever said that, though."

He knew what to do. Although his shoulder pulled, he leaned over and pressed a kiss to the side of

104

her breast, then another below it. "How long until O'Shea gets here?" he murmured against the tip of her nipple and was rewarded when it tightened in anticipation.

"Oh, Cyrus," Emily sighed, her hands finding his hair. She shifted. "It's early—eleven in the morning. Mr. O'Shea probably won't get here until two or three in the afternoon. Oh!"

Cyrus sucked her nipple into his mouth, teasing it with his tongue and teeth. "Good," he said as he kissed his way to her other breast. "Plenty of time." He licked the tight tip and then blew on it, drawing another gasp out of Emily.

Braced in his good arm, he had unfettered access to her body and the story it told. Freckles dusted her chest where the sun had kissed her over the years. She had a faint scar at the edge of her throat—a long, shallow cut. Had that been an accident? Or had someone hurt her?

"We cannot spend all day in bed," she said in a dreamy voice, stroking his hair. "I have things to do, Cyrus." She made no move to get up, however.

That was probably true. After all, he was still in hiding—even more so now that he had nowhere else to go. All he had was Emily. This morning, here with her in her bed, safely behind the locked door. Isaac was upstairs, Rob Boy and Beulah were safe and Dolly was being coddled and protected by ladies of the night.

He didn't know what would happen when Hank O'Shea showed up this afternoon. He didn't even know what would happen when Emily dressed and stepped through the door to become Mistress again. Would they ever get another time like this?

105

"Me," he told her, flexing his hips so that his hard cock dragged against the folds of her sex. "You have to do me."

The words felt odd in his mouth, to say such dirty things to Emily Franklin. There was still a part of him that saw her as the master's daughter. She had never been sweet and innocent—no one would claim that of her. She had known what went on around her father's plantation and she had railed against it. But back then, she had never been a sexual creature. She was to be spoken to with the utmost respect and discretion at all times. If anyone had told her then that they wanted to *do* her, it would not have ended well for them.

But that was then. He wasn't afraid of the consequences anymore. He had already had her and he was going to have her again, as many times as he could. He had a fleeting wish that he were still a younger man, that they were discovering this together for the first time.

The corner of her mouth ticked up into a sly grin. "Why, Cyrus Franklin! Are you importuning me? Scandalous. Simply *scandalous*."

He grinned and lowered his lips to her breast again. "You asked what I like last night. I like these." He nibbled and sucked until her back came off the bed and her hands gripped his hair. He ached to be inside of her, but he wasn't going to rush this. He couldn't fight the nagging feeling that this might be his best and only chance to loll away the morning with her. He would do everything in his power to make sure it wasn't, but just in case...

He wanted to commit every single moment to his memory.

Like the little gasp she made as he skimmed his teeth over the tight nub of her nipple or the way her hips shifted, grinding her sex against the head of his cock.

And the way she kept saying things like, "Well, I never!" or, "I do declare," in the thickest Georgia accent he'd ever heard, as if she were a virginal southern belle being introduced to sex for the first time.

And he never wanted to forget the sound of their laughter as it blended together.

As he played with her breasts, he slid a hand down and found the crease of her sex. Her giggles died away as he explored her most intimate folds. "Has it really been a year?"

"It has." She stroked his hair as he tested her flesh to see where it would give and where she would gasp. "Over the last several years—oh, *Cyrus*—" her breath caught in her throat as he found the little bud of her sex. "Yes, darling—right there. Ever since I saw you, I haven't—*oh*."

The truth of her words hit him. "How many since you saw me that first time? Because I haven't had anyone since I found you."

"No one?" She gasped again as he stroked his thumb over the bud of her sex. Then he slid two fingers inside of her and she writhed with the pleasure of it all.

"Nope. Had some offers, but they weren't you." More than a few offers, actually. A fair number of women he'd sheltered had taken a good look at him and what he had and decided that this was a place they could be happy. They'd offered to cook his meals and keep his house and have his children because they knew that he was a good man capable of love.

But he wasn't capable of loving them. His heart belonged to Emily—always had. And now his body belonged to her, too. He was an instrument of her pleasure.

He worked her body, relentlessly tormenting her bud and stroking into her body. Her legs tightened around his hand and she froze, her body as tight as a string. He could practically hear her vibrating as he dragged his gaze up. Her mouth was frozen in an *oh* of surprise and her eyes were glazed with lust. For the longest second, her body tightened and tightened more around his. Then her crisis broke and she collapsed back onto the bed, her chest heaving as if she had just won a great race.

"Oh, you darling man," she panted, leaning up to kiss him.

Slowly, he eased his fingers out of her body. "Yeah," he said, his voice thick with need. He hadn't disappointed her, but he needed to be deeper inside of her. He needed it now. "Yeah, I like doing that to you." His fingers were slick with her juices and, without breaking her gaze, he held them up to his mouth and licked. Her sweet cream exploded on his tongue. He wouldn't have thought it possible, but he got even harder.

She traced the tip of her own tongue over her lips. "What else do you like?"

It was hard to think through the haze of lust pounding through his head and his groin. A million fantasies crowded in his mind, all shoving for attention first.

"I want you to be completely honest," she said, pushing into a sitting position.

Cyrus shifted so that he was sitting on his heels, his erection jutting out from his body and demanding attention.

"You don't have to worry about shocking me." With that, she reached out and took hold of his shaft, encircling it with her fingers and thumb. She slid her hand up and then, at the tip, she gave a little squeeze this sent a shudder through his entire body.

He wanted her mouth around his cock and his name screamed from her lips. He wanted her on top, underneath him, beside him, and before him, her legs spread wide with everything on display. Yeah, that. He'd had his fair share of sex from behind but…

She squeezed him again before her hand slid back down, all the way to the base of his cock. With her other hand, she reached over and cupped his jewels. He moaned. He couldn't wait any longer. "On your knees."

She sucked in a little breath of air and his eyes flew open all the way. Had he shocked her?

No. Her eyes were dark with desire and she looked hungry again. "Do you know," she said, giving his cock one more squeeze before relinquishing her grip and turning to arrange the pillows, "that being taken from behind is one of my most favorite positions? Something about the way a good strong cock slamming into me feels…" She shivered. "You won't be gentle, will you?"

God, this woman. "Only if you want me to be."

She turned onto her knees, the pillows braced under her stomach. "Hard, Cyrus. Hard and rough and—"

It did things to him, hearing her say those dirty

things. He knelt between her legs, fitting the head of his cock against her crease. With one thrust, he was buried inside of her.

When he and Emily had made love last night, he'd done the best he could, but she had been in control. She had ridden him. He had gotten a good look at her breasts and her face, but he hadn't been able to see where their bodies had been joined.

Now he could. For an agonizing second, he couldn't move. Then, slowly, he began to withdraw, watching his shaft, glistening with her cream, emerge from her...

"What do you call this?" he demanded, ramming home again. "I'll use your word." Her crease, her slit, her netherlips, her—

"My pussy. Oh God, Cyrus. I love the feeling of your cock in my pussy." She moaned again, louder this time, and buried her face in the pillows.

Cyrus gripped her ass with his hands, his dark fingertips digging into her milky white flesh. He held her ass apart so that he could see even better when he sank into her. He was not gentle about it, but he didn't hurry, either. Every moment, there was another memory to learn. The way her back arched like a cat, the way she hid her cries in the pillows. The way her body took him in and squeezed him tight until he was almost out of his mind with the pleasure of it all.

It'd only been after she had freed him and all the other slaves, only after she had married that fool preacher, that Cyrus had allowed himself to think of her like this. And even then, he only did so in the deepest part of the night, as if darkness could hide his sinful thoughts.

But this? Although the draperies were drawn, light still filtered into the room. He withdrew again until only the very tip of his cock was still lodged in her body and then slammed home. The effort it took not to explode into her right now was monumental and he wouldn't be surprised if he wound up sleeping the entire day away after this. But he wasn't going to rush this along.

Again and again, his cock disappeared into her pink pussy.

"Anything, Cyrus," she moaned, thrashing against her pillows. "Anything for you."

He wanted to be more inside of her. Every way he could be inside of her, he wanted it. He skimmed his fingers over the tight bud of her asshole. "Anything?" Then he held his breath, afraid she would say no and equally afraid she would say yes.

"Fill me up, darling. But do be gentle there—at least for starters."

He almost laughed out loud. He withdrew from her pussy and stroked his fingers back into her sweet juices, coating his fingers. Then he replaced his fingers with his cock again and stroked his wet fingers over that tight bud. He eased a finger inside of her—Jesus, she was so tight. She gripped him and he almost came from that alone.

"Wait a second," she said in a whisper, panting hard. He almost withdrew, but she stopped him. "No, don't go—just give me a second to adjust. There." Even as she said it, he could feel the muscles relaxing, allowing him to slide his finger in deeper. "Yes, like that. You're going to make me come again, you know that?"

111

"To hear those words coming out of your mouth," he growled.

For a few hot moments, he slid his finger and his cock into her, reveling in the way her body responded to his, the way he could make her moan and writhe with pleasure.

"I can take in two fingers," she said, lifting her head. "I want to. I have some oil I use. And then I want you to stop being gentle. Smack my ass and make me come, Cyrus."

He eased free of her body. "*Woman.*"

She looked back over her shoulder and shot him that wicked grin. "Not today, but I'll even let you fuck me there. Or I have some objects I use. You can use them on me or I can use them on you."

His mouth dropped open as she leaned over and grabbed a small jar from the bedside table.

"Use this." She unscrewed the lid of the jar and Cyrus held out his hand. She dripped some of the oil, light and fragrant without being too runny, onto his hand and then went back to kneeling over the pillows, her legs spread wide. "I'm ready for you."

"You are everything I have ever dreamed of," he said as he spread the oil around her hole and slipped one finger inside again. He waited for that loosening of her muscles, withdrew his finger and this time, added the second. She moaned into her pillows again, her internal muscles clenching him and drawing them in deeper. "Yes," she hissed. "Like that. Now fuck me. Fuck me *hard*."

"Yes, ma'am." He buried his cock in her pussy again and did his level best to keep a steady rhythm with his hips and his hand. With his other hand, all he could do was hold on to her hip. He could tell that he was going to hurt when they were through, but oh, how this was worth the pain.

He surrendered to the pleasure of joining with Emily.

"God, Cyrus—*God*!" Emily cried out, thrashing underneath him. He felt all of her muscles tighten down on his fingers and his cock, and it was with relief that he followed her into the abyss of the climax. He pumped his hips until she had drained him dry.

Then his strength abandoned him and he fell forward, collapsing them both onto the bed. He managed to free his hand and withdrew from her body completely but for a long moment, they just lay there, breathing hard.

"I hope that was honest enough for you," he mumbled against the skin between her shoulders. "Haven't ever done that with anyone else. Not with the fingers."

She rolled until she could look him in the eye. "I like being your first—even if it's only for that." With a satisfied sigh, she reached out and stroked his face. "We need to get cleaned up and I have to go be Mistress. And you," she said, leaning up to kiss his forehead, "probably need a nap."

That was an understatement. Already, his arms felt like lead and he was having trouble keeping his eyes open.

Emily shoved his good shoulder. "You need to wash. Then you can rest while I take a bath and get ready."

He grumbled but managed to get up. He only swayed a little, which was progress. "Do I need to get dressed for O'Shea today? And can I see Isaac?" he called back into the room

"I'm not sure about Mr. O'Shea. He doesn't know why I asked him to come back. It wasn't safe to put the details down in a letter. But if enough of the girls go out this afternoon to do their shopping, then I should be able to take you up to the attic—providing you can get there on your own power and back again," she called back.

Cyrus washed his face and then washed everything else. Then another thought occurred to him. "Emily?"

"Yes, darling?"

"I didn't pull out. A child..."

She laughed, a light sound that had a forced edge to it. "Don't worry. I can't have children. No matter what the circumstance, I've never gotten with child." There was a tinge of sadness to her tone, one that he wondered if anyone else would notice.

He came out of the bathroom to find her reclined on his side on the bed, watching him. "All right, then."

She scowled at him. "I'm not very good with babies. I never have been. You know that. So don't pity me. I never wanted a baby."

He tried to shrug but his shoulder burned with the effort. "I don't have any kids, either. Just never worked out that way." That was one of the things Nadine back in Atlanta had wanted—a big family. Cyrus had cared for her a great deal and he liked kids. Always. But... it just never worked out that way. Nadine had left him for a sharecropper who had been widowed and already had two kids under the age of five. Last Cyrus had heard, Nadine had three more babies. He was glad she got her family.

Emily came to her feet. She looked almost nervous, he realized. "I know it's been years and years but I can't help but think that Dolly looks a little bit like my sisters."

That was what she said. But that wasn't all that Cyrus heard. As best he could, he stepped into her and wrapped his arms around her, chest to chest. The top of her head came almost to his nose and he breathed in the sweet smell of her hair. Her scent was of lemons, bright and clean. "Dolly does look like your sisters. And your sisters—they looked like you." In fact, he'd hazard a guess that Emily had already decided that Dolly looked like their child, if they could've had one by blood. As beautiful as Emily had been at that age, he could almost pretend that Dolly was the best part of both of them all mixed together.

A tremor passed through her body and then she was gone, pulling away from him and walking back to her private bath. "I can't keep her," she said, stopping at the door. "I'm going to send her away and if you're smart, Cyrus, you'll go with her." And with that, she shut the door.

Well.

That answered that question. She was still going to try and get him to leave due to some misguided notion of protecting him. But if she thought he was just going to go along with her little plans now that he finally had her, she had another think coming. He wasn't going to be so stupid as to walk away. He had made that mistake too many times in his life.

Whether she liked it or not, he was here to stay.

115

Chapter Nine

As a general rule, Emily did not get nervous. Anxiety and worry could be productive, if they drove her to take corrective action and right wrongs. And she had long since lost any sense of shame that would lead to embarrassment.

But as she watched the street from her office window, waiting for a glimpse of the imposing figure of Hank O'Shea to appear, she had to admit that she was nervous about this entire situation. She now had five people in this house who did not belong here. One she could hide successfully. Two she could hide reasonably well. But five? She shook her head.

Every minute Dolly and Cyrus were in this house was another minute all of their lives were at risk. Oh, how she longed for some mode of transportation that could get Dolly and Cyrus to Virginia City in a matter of days—hours, even. The trip by train would take weeks at best. Every stop would be another chance for Cyrus to change his mind and catch another train back to Brimstone.

Every stop would be a chance to hold him in her arms again. She shuddered, still able to feel the ghost of his fingers and his cock inside of her.

Her husband, God rest his soul, had not been

good in bed. With her years of experience, she wondered what their love life would've been like if he'd been honest with what he wanted. Looking back, she now suspected that he was the kind of man who would've enjoyed being bound and whipped. Many did. But no, that wasn't how a man of the cloth should carry on with his wife in the biblical sense, so instead they'd just had three miserable years of boring sex before he'd gotten himself killed.

Since then, she'd a great many lovers and a good many orgasms worth remembering. But they all paled in comparison to the release that Cyrus had unleashed upon her. Because with him, it wasn't just the physical act. It wasn't just about pleasure and satisfaction.

In her time, she'd scoffed at the concept of "making love" with another human. Love was an unknowable, unreachable ideal used to trap women into loveless marriages and other equally dire circumstances and she had been careful never to fall for it.

But for the first time, last night and then this morning, she had *made love* with a man. And it changed everything.

How was she supposed to send him away? She couldn't. But he couldn't stay with her, either.

Oh, what a mess this was.

Finally, she saw Hank O'Shea's broad figure strolling down the street. As best Emily could tell, Hank was a permanent third in the marriage of the former mayor of Brimstone, Raymond Dupree, and the woman once known as Miss Emerald Green—now Mrs. Emmeline Dupree.

Emmeline was supposed to have taken over the

117

Jeweled Ladies when Mistress retired, although when that was supposed to happen had never been clearly defined. Perhaps that was part of Emily's worry. She'd had a succession plan and now she didn't.

Regardless, Emily strongly suspected that Hank, Emmeline, and Raymond lived as a trio. Emmeline had never told Emily despite repeated prodding, but Emily was certain that Raymond preferred men and she knew that Hank preferred both. It made sense, in its own way. Raymond and Emmeline genuinely loved each other and Hank, well, he was the last man that Emily had invited to her bed. He was also one of the very few who had ever refused and for that, she liked him all the more. His loyalties were clear and they lay with the Dupree family.

But Hank O'Shea had also offered his help, should she ever need it. And, since he'd somehow found out about Emily Weatherspoon, he most likely knew a great deal of Emily's off-the-books activities. He could not be bought and he was not afraid of getting his hands dirty. In other words, he was exactly the sort of man she needed now. If anyone could get Cyrus out of this town in one piece, it was Hank O'Shea.

She checked the clock as she headed for the downstairs parlor. He was promptly on time. Cyrus had dozed away the greater part of the afternoon but after Emily had shooed everyone but Ruby out of the house, she had allowed him to walk upstairs to see his friends. They were to stay there until Ruby gave the all-clear. Emily figured she had less than an hour before the girls returned from their shopping trip and began to prepare for the evening crowd.

An hour in which to settle the fate of at least three people.

This was just another problem and she, along with Hank O'Shea, would arrive at some perfectly reasonable solutions. That was that.

It did not explain why, instead of letting Mr. O'Shea wait for her to make her grand entrance in the parlor, she rushed down the stairs to meet him. It did not explain why, when he took her hand and kissed her knuckles, her throat caught with unexpected, unwanted emotion. And it did not explain why, when he said, "Mistress, I'm yours to command," in his Irish brogue, she almost wept with relief.

Still, she had a part to play. If anyone should wander by, she and Hank needed to look like they were having an amorous conversation, not plotting a rescue mission. She brushed her hands over his shoulders and upper arms. "You're looking well. Life in Austin seems to agree with you. How is Emmeline? And the baby?"

Hank's hard face softened into a look of sheer joy as he pulled a small metal frame from an inside pocket. "They are well. Raymond is thriving in his new position and Emmeline has taken to society like you and I always knew she would." He held up the frame and Emily found herself looking down at a chubby-cheeked baby with raven black hair atop its head. "Sarah is just starting to talk. She's an absolute delight." He spoke with the pride of a father, not of a family friend.

Yes, it was as Emily had suspected. Hank was the girl's father, but Raymond gave her his name. "She's beautiful," Emily said, meaning it. "Do pass along my well-wishes to Emmaline and Raymond."

Hank bowed his head in acknowledgment and then turned the frame over. There was a family portrait of the Duprees—Raymond standing behind Emmaline and baby Sarah on her lap. This photo was older. Sarah was still in swaddling clothes.

"I'm so happy for her—for you all. Why aren't you in this photo?" It was as close as she had ever come to straight out asking.

Hank held her gaze for a moment, a twinkle in his eye. She knew and he knew that she knew, but she was unsurprised when he avoided the question completely. With one final long look at his family, Hank tucked the pictures back into his pocket, where he patted it. Emily was certain those photos went everywhere with him.

"Your letter seemed quite urgent," he began.

"I think this conversation would be better had elsewhere. Would you like to come upstairs?"

"The last time you asked me upstairs, it was not to go to your office."

Emily giggled, light and carefree when she felt anything but. "Sir, I would never break up a happy family. Any offer to my bedroom has been rescinded long since. This is a matter of some urgency, though, I need a man of your... skills." She leaned forward to run her fingers over his jaw. "However, if anyone asks, you did indeed come up to my bed."

Hank stood, grinning almost maliciously. "Indeed. And how was I?"

She laughed, leaning into him. His arm went around her waist. They understood each other very well. "Oh, you were fabulous, sir. This way."

"And you," he said as they worked their way

upstairs. "One of the best I've ever had, Mistress. The rumors were all true."

She laughed again, this time more deeply. Instead of leading him back toward the bedroom, she led him to the front. He'd been here once before and he settled into the seat with ease as she took her position behind the desk. "All right, now what's all this about?"

Only then did she allow herself to relax. "I have five unexpected guests in this house as we speak. Free Cyrus Franklin, an eleven-year-old mixed girl named Dolly, a giant, silent man who goes by Isaac and a colored husband and wife. The husband has been badly beaten and is struggling to hold onto his life."

Hank notched an eyebrow at her. "Not quite your usual clientele."

She shook her head. "It has not quite been my usual month." Quickly, she sketched in the details—Dolly's arrival, Cyrus's attempted murder, Ruby's retrieval of Isaac, Rob Boy and Beulah. However, she did not go into great detail about her long history with Cyrus. "They can't stay. I was going to send Dolly to Virginia City, where the former Brimstone schoolteacher resides with one of my former Jewels. They run a dress shop. Dolly would get her education and a trade while being raised by two women who care for her. But then Mr. Franklin had to go and get himself shot. Now he informs me that he won't leave."

Hank's gaze sharpened. "You, you mean? He won't leave *you*?"

If it were possible for her to blush after all these years, she might do so now. "That is correct."

Hank let out a long, low whistle. "I always wondered. Seemed like there was a lot more between

121

you two than met the eye." He studied her for a long second, but she refused to break. She was stronger than that. "So what's the problem?"

"If whoever set the trap for Mr. Franklin figures out he's still here, it will risk his life and mine, as well as every girl who lives here with me. I have to..." She swallowed, her throat tight. "I have to focus on the greater good. If I get him and Dolly away from here, we'll all be safer. And that's all I need. To know that they're safe."

Hank thought that over for a while. "You could go with them, you know."

Oh, it was so tempting. She could walk away from this life she'd made and start fresh. She had enough money to live out the rest of her days in luxury. Surely she and Cyrus could find someone willing to marry them. Then they could spend the rest of their days waking up together, being totally honest with each other in bed and out of it. They could raise Dolly as their own, the daughter she'd never had.

"It's not possible. Where would we go? I will not live the lie that he is my servant. There will always be people who make it their business to decide how I live my life. I've spent my whole adult life pushing back against those who would dictate my choices for me. Besides," she went on before Hank could object, "my replacement ran off and married the mayor. I don't know..."

At that moment, there came a brisk knock on the door. "Mistress?"

It was Ruby. "Come in."

Ruby stepped into the room and startled when Hank stood. "Oh, my. I'm sorry," she added. "I didn't know I was interrupting."

Hank bowed in her general direction. "I don't believe I've had the honor," he said smoothly.

Emily sighed. "Hank O'Shea, may I present Miss Ruby Red. She's been with me about a year, so I don't believe you would've had the opportunity to have made her acquaintance before. Ruby, this is Mr. Hank O'Shea. He is the assistant to our illustrious former mayor, Mr. Raymond Dupree. He has since been in Austin, continuing to serve Mr. Dupree in his capacity as the lieutenant governor."

Ruby quickly recovered herself, pasting on a charming smile and extending her hand so that Hank could brush his lips over her knuckles. "I definitely would've recalled meeting you, sir."

Emily rolled her eyes. "That's quite enough of that. Mr. O'Shea is here to help us deal with our houseguests." She turned her attention back to Hank, motioning for them both to sit. "Before she came to me, Ruby was, among other things, a nurse on Civil War battlefields. She is the only other person in this house besides Della and Samuel who knows for certain the number of guests we are currently lodging and where they are located. Among her many talents," she went on as Ruby stared at her, goggle eyed, "she also has the ability to dress and act as a man, which makes her extremely useful."

Hank weighed these options, looking at Ruby with new eyes. "I can see why Mistress values you so much. That and of course, your exceptional beauty. I am partial to redheads, myself. Are you Irish?"

Ruby glanced at Emily. "Mr. O'Shea, are you a paying gentleman caller?"

Emily snorted. "Absolutely not. Mr. O'Shea is here as a friend, offering assistance."

Ruby gave Hank a dull look. "No, I'm not Irish. Nor will I pretend to be for you. Happy?"

Hank chuckled. "Oh, I like you. I can see why Mistress put her faith in you. I trust that, if it's required later, you'll be able to pretend you at least tolerate me?" Ruby rolled her eyes at him. "Good." He turned his attention back to Emily. "Do you want suggestions or do you have a plan already in mind?"

"I need to get Cyrus out of this house. I was hoping that we could somehow get him and Dolly into the Dupree mansion. That is, if you don't mind having guests while you're in town?"

"I believe that Mr. Franklin's friend Isaac can take care of himself," Ruby added. "He's only still in the building because he's guarding Rob Boy and Beulah. Mr. Franklin is up in the attic with them now." Ruby thought for a moment. "It would be best to split Beulah and Rob Boy up but she won't leave him, so we'll have to make accommodations for that. In all honesty, I'm not sure he's going to make it. We need to be prepared for every outcome where Rob Boy is concerned."

Emily found herself staring at Ruby. With time and training, it was possible the woman would make an ideal replacement. Then, perhaps Emily could leave this town, this state. She could travel to Virginia City and reunite with Cyrus again. See with her own eyes how Dolly was growing up. And then...

She shook her head. Those dreams were just that—dreams. People in Virginia City would be no less welcoming of a white woman married to a black man than they were here. There was no good way for her and Cyrus to be together. Still, the idea of handing the Jeweled Ladies over to Ruby was one worth investigating.

"Excellent observations." She turned her attention back to Hank. "Well? Whoever set the trap wouldn't be expecting Mr. Franklin to be in the Dupree mansion. Once there, it'll be easier to get them out of town. "

Hank leaned his head back, staring into space somewhere to the left of Emily. "Can Mr. Franklin walk on his own power?"

"He made it up the stairs unaided." Ruby informed them. "He still needs a great deal of rest. I wouldn't recommend putting him on a horse just yet. But if you're asking whether or not he can walk out of this building under his own power, I believe he can."

Hank nodded his head once and stood, refocusing on Emily. "Do you have a rug that you feel comfortable sacrificing for the greater good?"

Emily was horrified. "You're not going to roll Mr. Franklin up in a rug and smuggle him out of here, are you?" He would absolutely *hate* that.

"Of course not," Hank said with another chuckle. "We're going to smuggle the girl out that way. Mr. Franklin will walk out of here with his head held high."

Chapter Ten

D o you think he's going to make it?" Cyrus kept his voice low, although there was no place to hide in the attic.

Isaac shot a worried look back to the safe room that Cyrus himself had recently occupied. The door was open and Beulah's legs stuck out. The noises coming from that room were not good and Cyrus could hear the woman praying mightily.

Isaac glanced back at Cyrus and shook his head. He mimed jostling and Cyrus understood. Getting Rob Boy out of the house before it burned and then getting him back to town had taken a toll on the man. Miss Ruby was doing the best she could, but…

"Mistress is meeting with Hank O'Shea. I think she's working on a plan to send me away."

Isaac looked relieved at that, which irritated Cyrus. The silent man had been with him for a couple of years and Cyrus trusted Isaac completely with everything but his connection to Emily.

"You may not be able to come with me," Cyrus warned. "I don't know what she's planning but…"

He wasn't going to leave her, but he didn't know how to explain to Isaac that he'd rather stay in a whorehouse with the most notorious madam in Texas

126

rather than cut and run to safety. He didn't know how he could stay hidden in this house, having to wait on the all-clear from Emily or Ruby before he did so much as set foot in the hallway. He also didn't know how he was going to let Emily send Dolly to an unknown fate, either. He couldn't stay and he couldn't go. All he knew for sure was that he couldn't live without Emily anymore. He was fifty-one, maybe fifty-two years old now. He'd spent a good thirty years thinking, *what if?* Well, no more.

He was done living with regrets.

"Mr. Franklin?" Cyrus turned to see Beulah, her cheeks tear-stained and her hands twisted in her apron. "Can you fetch Miss Ruby? He…" her voice caught in her throat as she looked back at the small room where Rob Boy most likely lay dying. A rough gurgling noise seeped out of the room. "He don't sound too good."

"Yes, ma'am." He patted her on the shoulder. It never got any easier, when someone made it as far as the sanctuary of his home only to succumb. That's what had brought Isaac to him. He'd come after a soiled dove who'd been cut real bad. Cyrus had dug her grave because Isaac hadn't been able to do anything other than sit with the dove's body. Isaac had loved that girl. Beulah loved her Rob Boy. Only death could've separated them from their beloveds and only death could keep him from Emily. It was that simple.

Now he just had to convince her of that.

Emily had sent everyone except Ruby out so Cyrus had permission to leave the attic when he saw fit. Nonetheless, he nearly ran in to Ruby at the bottom of the steps.

"Mistress would like to speak to you," she said, flashing him a brilliant smile.

He didn't trust that smile because it was a Jewel's smile and he liked to think he'd gotten to know this odd woman a little better than that. Still, he was glad to see her because he'd rather leave the doctoring to Ruby. "Beulah sent me for you, anyway. She thinks Rob Boy's getting worse."

Ruby sighed, her smile falling away. "He doesn't need a doctor, he needs a priest. But I'll do my best."

"Thank you."

Ruby turned to sidle past him but Cyrus caught her by the arm. "Where's Dolly?"

This time, Ruby's smile reached her eyes. "She's in the kitchen with Della. Mistress found her a slate and some chalk and they're working on the important words."

Cyrus dropped his hand away from her arm. "The important words?"

"Sure. Her name, her age, please, thank you, milk, cookies—everything a little girl needs to know."

Cyrus couldn't help himself. He chuckled. Dolly should know some sweet words. "That's good. That's real good."

"Mistress is going to send her away. She's not going to keep that girl."

Ruby's statement hung in the air because what she didn't say was almost as important. Mistress wasn't going to keep Cyrus either.

"Down to the second floor, all the way to the front of the house—that's her office," Ruby called over her shoulder as she headed upstairs.

Cyrus got his first good look at the second floor

of the Jeweled Ladies and everything he saw made his heart sink. It wasn't just Emily's room that had every luxury. It was the whole house. The rug in the hallway was plush and soft underfoot—no rag-rugs or dirt floors here. The woodwork was oiled until it gleamed and the frames around the art and mirrors, because of course Emily had both on display everywhere, were gilt.

He'd heard this place was the fanciest place in Texas but he'd always pictured the Big House from the Franklin plantation when he'd thought what the interior of the Jeweled Ladies brothel would look like. This was so much more than that.

He'd invested wisely the money Emily had given him and he'd worked for the rest. Compared to his way of living growing up, he'd come up a great deal in the world. But this?

He couldn't compete with Emily's luxuries.

He made his way to her office. There was something familiar about walking through a grand home where he didn't belong, having been called in to talk to Emily. The specter of death still lurking in the corners. And of course, Emily deciding his fate for him.

He paused outside her office door, trying to get his thoughts in order. She was not sending him away and that was *final*.

Thirty years ago had been different. He'd known that she was going to give him his freedom. Cyrus had been the last one called up to the Big House. By then, half the freed slaves had already packed up their things and their new wealth and set out for a better life. Every single one of them had been given a portion of the payment Emily had taken for selling the plantation out from under her uncle's nose. Forty-nine slaves—no, that hadn't been true anymore—forty-nine freed men and women had suddenly found themselves not only free, but in the possession of about two hundred dollars each. The ones who'd had their families sold away from them got a little bit more. The ones who had been permanently scarred by her father had gotten the most. But no one went away empty-handed. Cyrus had even seen some people carrying out furniture or candlesticks—mementos? Or things to be sold? Emily obviously hadn't cared. In all honesty, Cyrus had been surprised she hadn't burned the plantation to the ground and salted the earth.

He'd walked into that library which had been her father's office, but was now hers. He'd dared to hope that, in addition to being suddenly free and wealthy, that he and Emily could be together. He had been twenty-one or twenty-two—never had a birthday before. And Emily had been eighteen, full of righteous vengeance and, through some legal chicanery, the sole possessor of the Franklin Estates plantation.

Even then, she had been comfortable wielding her power. A slip of a girl still, she'd sold the plantation and made reparations, leaving herself practically penniless. She'd been ready to leave. Cyrus had been planning on going with her.

What he had not expected was finding a man in the office, not behind the desk in the seat of power, but standing by the window. An older man with thinning hair and a bit of a belly. But for all that, he had kind eyes and an easy smile as Emily had introduced him as the Reverend Phineas Weatherspoon, her husband.

The revelation had hit him like a punch to the gut, but even then, Cyrus would've gone with her. He would've watched them live as husband and wife, because it still would've been enough just to be close to her. He could've protected her.

He had all but begged. The only reason he hadn't fallen to his knees was because of the pitying look Phineas Weatherspoon had given him. In that moment, Cyrus had hated him more than any man alive and almost as much as Chester Franklin, who was thankfully dead.

Cyrus shook back to himself. That sense of the familiar had the hair on the back of his neck standing up as he turned the handle and walked into the sunlight-flooded room. Because there was Emily, seated behind the desk in the position of power. And there was a man standing by the window, a man who looked at Cyrus with kind eyes and a gentle smile.

Cyrus's teeth were on edge. He would *not* beg. But he would not take her money and walk out of this house because she thought it was for the best, dammit. When he had received his freedom, it had made sense to go along with all the big ideas Emily had been espousing—freedom for the slaves, teaching the native Indians to read and bringing them Christianity. She'd decided to save the world from itself and Cyrus had been a slave for all of his life, except for twenty minutes of it. He hadn't known how to go on then. Negotiating the world as a free black man was something he'd had to learn on his own. So when she'd sent him away, he'd gone because he'd trusted that she'd known best.

But he was older, and he liked to think, wiser

131

now. Emily wore her power even more easily than she had thirty years ago, but he'd come up in the world. And he wasn't going to let her push him away again.

"Franklin," Hank O'Shea said coming forward with his hand out. "Good to see you again."

That much, at least, had changed in the last thirty years. Phineas Weatherspoon, while polite and genial, had not shaken Cyrus's hand during their brief interview. Cyrus had always wondered if Emily's intended saw how much Cyrus had been in love with her? Could O'Shea see the same thing now? Cyrus didn't care.

"O'Shea," he replied, trying to sound calm when he wasn't. There was too much of the past mixed up with his present. "Have you two been plotting?"

Emily's gaze sharpened as she motioned for him to take a seat. "Plotting is a harsh word, Mr. Franklin."

He rolled his eyes at her. Were they back to this again?

"We have, however, been discussing the future. The immediate future."

He settled into the chair, rooting himself to it. He'd like to see her pry him out of it. And then, because Emily obviously trusted Hank enough to bring him in here, he said, "Whose future, Emily? Mine? Dolly's? Yours?"

Her nostrils flared with displeasure when he used her name, but he couldn't care.

Hank sat down in the other chair. He looked like he was enjoying himself. "Careful," he said in a stage whisper. "I hear she's a pretty good shot."

She turned an increasingly powerful glare on Hank. "I wouldn't recommend testing me. Either of you. Yes,

Cyrus." He grinned when she used his name, which only made her madder. "We have been discussing your future. You cannot stay at the Jeweled Ladies. And neither can Dolly. I believe Mr. O'Shea—"

"We're all friends here," he interrupted, his accent suddenly stronger. "Call me Hank, Emily."

"I take it you've filled him in on some of the gaps?" Cyrus asked her.

Hank paused at that, his gaze darting between the two of them. Emily continued to glower and Cyrus recalled the few times he had seen her throw a fit back on the plantation. Of course, even then, she'd been different. Instead of pitching a tantrum over a pony or a new dress, she'd damn near cowed her own father with the strength of her anger when she'd caught him whipping a child for stealing a piece of bread, if Cyrus recalled correctly. There'd been a line of some Shakespearean play she had read to him once— something about being fierce yet tiny. That was his Emily, always had been. But he doubted she would appreciate the reference right now.

"I have a good grip on the present," Hank finally admitted, breaking the silence. "Not too sure how you two came to be together, though..." He let his voice trail off, as if either Cyrus or Emily would rush to fill in the gap.

Cyrus looked at her. She arched an eyebrow, looking imperial, and almost smiled. She wasn't going to tell and neither was he. "We have a plan to get you out of the house," she said to Cyrus, ignoring Hank's affected look of insult. "From there, it'll be easier to get you out of town."

"No."

The word settled over the room like a damp fog.

"Cyrus—"

"*No*, Emily. I have already told you once. More than once. You're not sending me away. You don't get to make this decision."

"I can't keep you here," she said, her voice cracking on the words. "Don't you see that, you damn fool? Someone tried to kill you. If they find you—"

Yeah, he knew all that. He still didn't care. "Come with me. I'll go if you come along. We could even keep Dolly." He leaned forward, putting his hands on the desk. His wound pulled but it hardly hurt. How could it, when he saw the look of longing in her eyes? "We could be a family, Emily."

Her eyes grew bright and then, abruptly, she stood and turned her back to them. He thought he heard her mutter, "you damn fool," a few more times under her breath, but it wasn't clear if she was talking about him or herself.

Cyrus looked at the man sitting on his right.

"For the record," Hank said. "I asked the same question. I don't recall getting a satisfactory answer."

"Go to hell," Emily said in a quiet yet unmistakable voice. "Where would we go? Can either of you answer me that? Is there a single place in this country—this continent—where we could go and live out this fantastical dream of yours, Cyrus? How long would it be before disaster struck? Before someone figured out who I was or who I used to be. Before someone decided that it just wasn't right that a black man and a white woman should live together as husband and wife? How long would it be before they came for Dolly?"

134

"Then we'll go somewhere where there aren't people. It's a big country. Lots of space. And I don't need anyone but you, Emily. Why do you think I've hung around this godforsaken stretch of Texas for the last seven years? Why do you think I've risked my neck to come to town just for a glimpse of you? Because you are the most important person in the world to me. Even when you won't talk to me. Even when you won't look at me. It doesn't change things." He stood and walked over to her, leaning his shoulder into hers. "I'm not going without you. You can't make me."

"I could shoot you," she said, her voice wavering. "Just a flesh wound. And then, while you're too weak to fight, I could have Mr. O'Shea haul you away."

"I'd come back, you crazy woman."

"I prefer you not shoot him," Hank said in a mild voice. "He looks heavy."

They ignored him.

"That's it?" Emily demanded, her voice more level. "Run away to the wilderness? That's your solution?" She shook her head. "Cyrus, may I remind you that I've done that already? Oh, I know it would be different this time. The native peoples have been decimated by sickness and war. And you wouldn't get yourself killed like Phineas did." She held up a hand, cutting off his protest. "How long do you think I would last? I have lived my entire life, except for about three years, in fine homes with servants and cooks. I have spent twelve years here, with hot water that runs in pipes and the town at my feet, eager to give me whatever I desire. French silks. Persian carpets. Oriental vases." She turned to him, her eyes blazing. "Trains come to

135

Brimstone because I demanded it." She glanced back at Hank, now cutting him off. "Yes, I am aware that both Mayors Dupree fought for the trains as well and that they serve the cattle barons as much, if not more, than they serve me. But don't tell me you aren't aware of my involvement."

Hank held up his hands in surrender. "Your investments sealed the deal. I know that. And you made a pretty penny off the railway, too."

She ignored this, but Cyrus was surprised. She really was the most powerful woman in Texas, wasn't she?

"I could make it work for a year, maybe two," she went on. "And maybe it's vain and selfish, but I'm telling you Cyrus—I can't do it. I couldn't do it when I was twenty. I'm almost 50 now."

He tangled his fingers with hers. She sniffed and he fished a worn handkerchief out of his pocket and handed it to her.

"Besides," she went on after a moment. "We could tromp out to the middle of nowhere, somehow scrape together a hardscrabble existence where every day we fight for survival and then they'll discover gold in the next mountain over and our quiet, hidden existence will be shattered. We cannot hide who we are."

"There has to be a way. I won't accept that fate has brought us back together again just to rip us apart. You're Mistress, Emily. You're rich and powerful and brilliant and ferocious and I cannot believe that you would accept sending me away as the only viable solution. I'm not going to."

"I need you to leave the brothel, Cyrus." Her

voice caught and tears began to stream down her face. "If it were just you and me or even the two of us and Dolly... But people rely on me. Just like they rely on you. Your friend and those poor people in the attic and my girls. All of the women that I have helped over the years. People need me."

He stared at her, rage beginning to burn in his chest. Was she serious? Of course she was. "I need you. And I'm done waiting for you."

For the longest second, she held his gaze and he thought she was going to bend. He didn't want her to break, but there had to be some bend to her.

Then, with a gentle shake of her head, she pulled her hand away from him. "For my safety, you're going to leave this place. You're going to do what Hank tells you. You're going to stay in the Dupree mansion for the time being. And maybe..." Her back straightened. "Perhaps a solution will present itself while you're there. But Cyrus, if you can't come up with a solution—if *I* can't come up with a solution," she quickly added when he opened his mouth to point out that she had to want it, too, "when it's time for Dolly to go to Virginia City, you *will* go with her."

Cyrus stared at her. He didn't know whether to laugh or cry or punch something.

"I suspect you'll be in the Dupree mansion for a couple of weeks," Hank offered gently.

Cyrus startled. He'd almost forgotten about the other man listening in on what should have been the most private of conversations.

"I believe I've recently inherited a large amount of money and I've come back to Brimstone to celebrate with the finest that money can buy. Can't

137

stand all the cooing Raymond and Emmeline are doing with that baby of theirs. I needed a break." He stood. "I believe I will be requesting private audiences with Mistress in the mansion while I'm here. That way, you two can see each other."

The fact that they even had to frame this as Hank having an affair with Emily stuck in Cyrus's gullet. "And the girl?"

"I'll get her over there, too. Leave it to me."

Cyrus turned his attention back to Emily, who was staring out the window as if her life depended on it. He thought she was just going to pretend he wasn't there like she had done for years on the street, but when he turned to go she said quietly, "Cyrus, I'm not giving up on you. I just can't see the way forward."

"Keep looking." With that, he walked away from her.

Chapter Eleven

In the end, Dolly did not get smuggled out in the carpet. The earthly remains of Rob Boy were instead wrapped in a worn rug and carried out by Samuel and Isaac the next day. Isaac then got in the cart with Rob Boy's body in the back and headed west to bury him near where Cyrus's house used to stand.

Beulah was inconsolable, but Emily knew that the woman needed to keep moving. If she spent all her time looking back at what she'd lost, she'd never survive and that was another problem to solve. Emily sent out letters to her usual contacts, but she didn't worry about sneaking Beulah out of the house. Women came and went all the time. In the meantime, she put Beulah in the kitchen with Della. At the very least, Della would keep the grieving widow busy and sometimes, that was just enough to go on.

Emily had not known Rob Boy, but his death saddened her in ways she hadn't expected. It was bad enough that a man had lost his life and left behind a woman who had cared for him. Worse that he'd been attacked because he'd been black. But beyond those tragedies, Emily couldn't help but see Rob Boy's murder as anything but a stark reminder about what awaited her and Cyrus if they tried to make a life together.

You could go with him.

For Hank O'Shea, the situation was exactly that clear. Emily could send him away, she could keep him here, or she could go with him. Three simple choices when it was anything but. Even a woman of her considerable power and wealth couldn't fight against the larger forces of racism and hatred. God knew she had been trying for years and years, but...

Two days after Rob Boy was carted away to his final resting place, Hank O'Shea waltzed into the Jeweled Ladies late in the evening. He was, to the naked eye, roaring drunk. His clothes were disheveled and he reeked of bad whiskey. He brought with him a black man, tall and broad with a shy smile. Hank told anyone who would listen about how the black man had saved him from being set upon by robbers outside of one of the other saloons and he was going to pay back his new friend with style and that meant a night at the Jeweled Ladies. The finest money could buy.

The black man was actually a Pinkerton agent by the name of Donald Shane and Hank had assured Emily that the man could get into or out of any house, as the case may be.

Hank and Mr. Shane settled into the saloon side of the brothel, Hank losing insane amounts of money in a card game. Ruby found her way into Hank's lap and Opal took hold of Mr. Shane. Emily kept an eye on them while keeping her distance.

Finally, Hank swooped Ruby into his arms and stumbled for the stairs. Opal dragged Mr. Shane along behind them, promising that he was going to see something he'd never seen before. And given Opal's reputation within the Jeweled Ladies, the foursome got more than their fair share of lascivious glances and knowing smirks.

Exhibitionists, Emily thought.

After that, she couldn't keep an eye on what was happening, but she knew the plan. In Ruby's room, Cyrus and Mr. Shane would trade clothing. Opal would try to seduce both Hank and Mr. Shane and fail miserably. She would settle for making a lot of noise, as if there were four people engaged in athletic bed play. Ruby would give Mr. Shane a copy of the file that Emily had of everything she had on Junie and Liza and then the man would slip out of the house, unseen.

There had been a long discussion about whether or not Mr. Shane should also spirit Dolly out, but Emily had eventually decided it was not worth the risk of them being caught together. She couldn't bear to watch another black man die.

The minutes ticked by interminably as Emily swanned around her parlor and saloon, making sure all of her gentlemen callers were well satisfied with whatever diversions they had chosen to spend their money on that evening—drink, cards, women. At this point in the evening, most people who were going to fuck a whore had already done so and the ones who were left were focused on poker or blackjack. A few were waiting their turn, but most of the girls were in rooms with gentlemen.

The exception was Miss Turquoise Sky, the beautiful young native girl who hadn't yet decided if she was going to whore or not. She didn't speak English fluently, but Miss Sky had, at some point, learned guitar. She sat on the raised stage at one end of the saloon, playing every known melody she'd ever heard. She sometimes sang along, although her lyrics were more sounds than actual words. Miss Sky had quite a talent and, frankly, if she decided not to pursue whoring, Emily was tempted to keep her on just for her musical talents.

Garnet made her way back into the saloon, clearly hoping to pick up another gentleman in the waning hours of the night. Sterling, the bartender, was wiping down the bar.

The hour seemed to last forever. What were they doing up there, for heaven's sake?

Finally, seemingly still drunk as a skunk, Hank stumbled downstairs with a reasonable facsimile of Mr. Shane behind him. Emily knew that it was Cyrus, but then again, she'd been able to pick him out on the midnight black street. Hopefully, no one else recognized the differences between the two men. Cyrus wore Mr. Shane's hat pulled low over his eyes.

She kept her distance but Cyrus looked up and their gazes locked. He touched the brim of Mr. Shane's hat with his fingers and Emily inclined her head.

Then he and Hank O'Shea walked out of the Jeweled Ladies and Emily had to fight the ridiculous urge to cry.

There had to be a way forward.

But what?

Cyrus was in the library with Dolly, reading a newspaper spread out on the desk before them, when the knock came.

"I'll get it," Hank said with a grin. He rose from the wingback chair he'd been sitting in and headed toward the door.

Dolly clutched at Cyrus's sleeve. "Should we hide?"

"No, honey. It's either Mistress Emily or Miss Ruby. And if it's not either one, then Hank won't let them in. Let's just be quiet," he finished with a whisper as the front door creaked open.

He could hear Hank talking, although he couldn't make out the words through the thick walls. He was pretty sure he heard a lighter, softer voice, but he couldn't tell if it was Emily's or not.

It had been three days since he had slipped out of the Jeweled Ladies dressed in another man's clothes. Three days since he had exchanged one prison for another. True, staying at the Dupree mansion was hardly like being imprisoned at all. He had his own room—so did Dolly—and, as long as he did not light a lamp while Hank was out and about town, he could go anywhere he wanted in the house. He could cook his meals his own way. Hank made *terrible* coffee.

He and Dolly had taken to spending most of their time in the library. The girl was quick-witted and intelligent. She could already pick out easy words and was getting to the point where she might soon start making out whole sentences. Teaching her was a productive use of his time and energy, but even then, it hadn't stopped his mind from wandering back to Emily.

There *had* to be a way. But what? She was right—living on the far edge of the frontier wasn't a long-term solution and a town or even a big city, like New York came with too much risk. Where could they go?

The voices got louder and Cyrus heard the front door creak shut. Dolly clutched his sleeve with both

143

hands but then Hank entered the room, a friendly smile on his face and behind him—

"Mistress," Dolly exhaled in relief.

Cyrus stood, inadvertently pulling Dolly to her feet, too. When Emily saw him, her eyes lit up and even though it had been three long, frustrating days without her around to even argue with, he felt something loosen in his chest.

He stood taller. "Mistress." A flash of something that he wanted to believe was longing came and went so quickly over her face that he almost missed it.

"Mr. Franklin," she said in her most prim voice. Hank snorted with amusement before Cyrus got the chance to. "And how are you today, Miss Dolly?"

"I like it here," she said. "This is a real nice place and Mr. Cyrus is teaching me to read. He says I'm good at it." She thought for a moment. "Miss Della makes better cookies, though."

Emily stood very straight, not moving. She looked almost pained at this recitation of facts. "She does, doesn't she? Come, dear. I wanted to come see you sooner, but I couldn't get away." She moved to the settee and sat down, arranging her skirts around her. Then she patted the spot next to her and Dolly sat.

"I wish we had more time," Emily said, reaching over and tucking a short lock of Dolly's hair behind her ear. "But soon, you'll be on your way to Virginia City, where Miss Minerva and Miss Abigail will take you in. Miss Minerva will continue to teach you how to read and do your figures and Miss Abigail will teach you how to sew beautiful, beautiful dresses. Why, I can even arrange for you to have singing lessons. Won't that be wonderful?"

Hank ducked out of the room and part of Cyrus wanted to follow because this wasn't right. He meant what he'd said in her office. They didn't have to send this girl away.

Cyrus had had lovers, but he had never been able to give them what they wanted—a family. His heart. He couldn't because no matter the time, no matter the distance, his heart belonged to Emily.

He liked kids. Children were proof that life went on, no matter how dark the times seemed. Dolly was proof. She'd never been a slave, and God willing, she never would be.

Emily reached out and took Dolly's hand in hers. "Don't be sad, dear," she said in a soft voice. "It will be exciting. You'll get to ride steam locomotives and carriages and when you get there, Miss Abigail will make you new clothes, just for you. It will be perfect. You'll see." She sounded like she was trying to convince herself and failing.

Dolly's head dipped and Cyrus could see her thin shoulders quivering. "I can't stay here with you and Mr. Franklin?" she asked in a tiny voice. "He's real nice, too. We could even be a family."

If possible, Emily's back got even straighter. She glared at him—him!—over the top of Dolly's head, as if he had put the girl up to this. He had done no such thing.

"I just don't see how we can make that work," she said gently. "Your future is too important to me to let you be raised in an establishment such as mine. You're a good girl. You're going to grow into a proper young woman. I'm doing what I can to make sure you have the best available to you." She shot Cyrus a look that dared him to contradict her.

145

He came to stand behind the couch and rested one of his hands on Dolly's head. "It'll work out," he told the girl because he had to believe it. He had lived his entire life grasping at that simple bit of hope. Somehow, it would all work out. And when he'd found Emily seven years ago, he had dared to think that finally, it would.

He didn't want to be wrong in this.

Dolly's eyes watered. Emily gave her hand a brisk pat and said in an equally brisk voice, "Show me what you've learned thus far."

Dolly gathered up the newspaper that she and Cyrus had been studying. Cyrus decided he couldn't watch them together anymore. He wanted to hold onto every memory he could, but this was too much even for him.

He had turned to go when Emily spoke to him.

"Mr. Franklin, I would hope that, after I get done hearing about Dolly's progress, that I might have a… private word with you before I leave?"

His body jumped to attention immediately even as he stared at her in disbelief. Did she want to talk or did she want fuck? And did it matter? Their time together was growing short and he still didn't have a workable solution to the seemingly insurmountable problem. He might want to wring her pretty little neck, but he wasn't sure he could pass up another opportunity to be with her.

"Of course." As he walked out of the room, his gaze fell upon a large, round object in the corner of the room he hadn't really noticed before.

A globe. A map of the whole entire world.

Back in the kitchen, Hank had brewed some

terrible coffee and arranged some not-terrible cookies on a tray.

"I don't know what to do," Cyrus said, staring into a cup of brown water. At least it was hot, even if a body couldn't call it 'coffee' in good conscience.

"What are your options?"

Cyrus got the feeling that, no matter what he'd been talking about, Hank would've said the same. "I don't think I can let that girl make the trip to Virginia City by herself. Maybe…" It felt like a defeat to even say this out loud. "Maybe I should go along with Dolly, make sure she gets settled. And then I could come back?" There was a thought rattling around the corners of his brains, which he couldn't quite get a handle on just yet.

Hank shrugged. "Sounds risky, at least until we figure out who shot you."

Cyrus rotated his shoulder. It was getting better, but he still wouldn't want to pick a fight with anyone.

"I'll go out tonight," Hank went on, "see what I can find out over a poker game or two. Someone in this town knows something."

Cyrus nodded his head in appreciation. "Be careful, man. You've taken up with Mistress and someone shot me in front of her place. It won't take a genius to put one and one together and come up with two."

Hank snorted and dumped the rest of his terrible coffee down the sink. "This town is perilously short of geniuses. You work on your problem from your end and I'll work on it from mine."

Cyrus dropped his head into his hands. Hope was a powerful thing. It had kept him alive through some dark times. But this? "She's right—that's the problem. There's no place we can go in this country or this continent that would be safe enough."

Hank came to stand next to Cyrus and put a hand on his good shoulder. "You know," he said in a deceptively light voice, "there's more than one continent in this world."

Hank's words went off like a bomb inside Cyrus's head. The globe! The one in the corner of the library that showed where all the countries of the world were located! He was not unseemly rich, but he'd saved his money and managed to turn hard work and Emily's two hundred dollars into a couple of thousand that he kept safely in a bank in New York City. And Emily… God only knew how much money she had. More than enough to buy passage on a boat. They could leave this country behind.

Why hadn't he thought of it? They could go anywhere. See the world. There would be limits, of course. Not everywhere would be different from here. But there had to be somewhere where they could live.

"I'll keep our young friend focused on her studies. Do you want me to send Mistress to the kitchen or…" Cyrus shook back to himself and saw Hank standing in the doorway to the kitchen, a smile that would've been an irritating smirk if he hadn't just changed Cyrus's entire life.

"I'll fetch her myself. That and your *globe*."

Chapter Twelve

Cyrus," Emily said sharply. "Calm down and tell me what you're talking about. I can hardly understand you." She had thought she'd come to visit with Dolly and spend a stolen hour with this man in bed. Instead, he had burst into the library, grabbed a globe and hauled her away from Dolly. He had all but ran up the stairs into a bedroom, which was home to a very nice bed that she wouldn't mind using, but instead he'd plunked her down in a chair and sat the globe before her. He was spinning it loudly and talking about... continents? "I don't need a geography lesson, darling."

"Obviously, Antarctica is out. I don't fancy penguins. Are there penguins in Antarctica? And I'm not sure about Africa. It's a large continent," he babbled as the globe continued to spin. "I suppose you could make an argument that it would be a homecoming of sorts. But I don't know where my people came from and that doesn't seem the sort of thing a Pinkerton agent would specialize in, you know?"

"Cyrus," she said even more harshly this time. She reached out and stopped the globe from another rotation. "What are you talking about? Penguins? I thought we..."

"A solution, Emily." He practically vibrated with energy. "Why didn't I think of it before? It's obvious. You're right." His eyes were bright—almost fevered with enthusiasm.

"Well," she said, wondering if she should be afraid. "It's about time you realized that I usually am."

"How much money do you have? I mean, all told? I got about seven hundred dollars buried out by my house and about another two thousand or so in a bank in New York City. That would be enough, don't you think?"

She stared at him in disbelief. It was as if he was stuck in a mania. Maybe she should slap him? "*Cyrus*. Enough for what?"

He twirled the globe with so much force that she had no choice but to let it spin again. He stuck a finger down on it hard enough to stop the rotation. "Here?"

"Anytime you want to start making sense, you just let me know." But she looked at where he was pointing. "The middle of Europe? What's there?"

"France." He said the word as if it contained the secret of life. "They have colonies in Africa, don't they? But they abolished slavery a long time ago, didn't they? There's black people in France. And aren't they supposed to all be libertines or something?" Unexpectedly, he fell to his knees next to her and took her hands in his. "Marry me, Emily. You are the only woman I have ever loved and I have been yours, heart and soul, my entire life. Be my wife and we'll take Dolly with us. We can be a family, finally—after all these years. Just say you'll be mine."

She really should slap him. He wasn't making a damned bit of sense. "What's in France?" she asked slowly, clutching his hands harder.

150

"*Us*, Emily. You and me. We can buy passage on a ship and set sail. It doesn't have to be France," he hurried to add when her mouth fell open in shock. "England abolished slavery, didn't they? Before we did, anyway. Maybe we could go there. Anywhere you want. China. Russia—although Russia will be cold."

"You're babbling again," she murmured, unable to do anything but gape at him.

"We don't even have to get married," he offered. "But you're right. There's no place in this country—this continent—where you and I can live the way we want to without worrying that every day would be our last. But there are other continents, Emily. Other *countries*, with different values and different histories. Countries where you'll never be the infamous Mistress and I'll never be just a freed slave. Think of it, Emily—we could start fresh, with Dolly as our daughter."

She blinked. Then, she blinked again. There was a roaring in her ears and the room had begun to blur and she was sure she wasn't hearing him correctly. The air seemed to be crackling with electricity. A storm must be blowing in. It was the only explanation for the sensations swamping her. "...*France*?"

"Wherever. I don't care where we go. It's a big world and all I want is one little part of it to be with you."

It was not the first time she had ever been proposed to. It wasn't even the twentieth. But Cyrus Franklin, on his knees, had just made the most crazed and the most romantic statement of love she had ever heard. "Do you think..."

"You're the most powerful woman in Texas," he

151

reminded her, as if she would ever forget. "You bend the men of this state to your will. You run a network of spies and informants. You probably have more money than I can even comprehend. Who says we have to stay here? Unless…" For the first time, the excitement in his eyes dimmed and he leaned back, pulling his hands free of hers. With some difficulty, he climbed to his feet. "Unless you don't want to give up Mistress. I know you have responsibilities." He took a step back as if bracing for the blow. "I know it's your life."

The roaring in her ears only got louder. Her chest tightened and she had trouble breathing. What did she know of France? The French made great soap and even better dresses.

But then there'd been Madame Colette, Emily's mentor. Hadn't she always bemoaned the strict sense of propriety that Americans clung to? Emily tried to recall what Madame Colette had thought about black men. If they had the coin, she was thrilled to fuck them. But was that easy acceptance a reflection of French attitudes at large or just a business opportunity a good madam refused to pass up?

Would she and Cyrus be safe in Paris? Would they be able to raise Dolly without interference or intimidation?

"I don't know," she murmured out loud, staring at the small square labeled *France* on the globe.

Cyrus made a noise that sounded like he was in pain. Startled, she looked up at him. "I just thought… It was a solution." His shoulders sagged. "But if you're not interested…"

Oh, she was making a total mess of this. She all but threw herself out of the chair, knocking the globe to the side. It fell onto the carpeting with the thud, but she didn't even stop to see if it had broken. She'd buy a new one, if it had. Instead, she launched herself at Cyrus in a completely undignified and unladylike way. She threw her arms around his neck and hauled him down into a kiss so hard that she was afraid she split his lip. She'd buy him a new lip. That thought was so ridiculous that she started to giggle, but she didn't stop kissing him.

For an agonizing second, he didn't kiss her back and she was terrified that she had already ruined everything. But then, with a grateful sigh, his arms came around her waist and he clutched her to him was a growl of satisfaction.

"You damn fool," he muttered against her lips, his hands already searching for her buttons.

"I know," she said, pulling away far enough that she could get the buttons of his trousers open. She was right and she was a damn fool and she was both things at the same time because why hadn't she thought of it? After all, Madame Colette had taught her how to kiss like the French, to fuck like the French. Madame Colette had often bemoaned the strict rules and divisions of the American society.

France. It was the perfect solution.

"Emily," Cyrus groaned as her fingertips brushed his engorged cock. "Let me—"

She fell to her knees and freed his cock. It sprang out from his thatch of black hair, eager for her touch. "No. You let me." She wrapped both hands around his shaft and stroked slowly up and back down.

Cyrus groaned and sagged against the bedpost. "Woman—God, Em."

153

In the scant week that they had together in the Jeweled Ladies, she had had him in all of the important ways except this one. She leaned forward and pressed an almost chaste kiss to his tip. His cock jerked in her hand as if it knew what it needed.

She stroked him once more, looking up at him from where she knelt on the floor. He was staring at her, that excitement back in his eyes. Without breaking his gaze, she leaned forward and took him in her mouth.

His mouth fell open as his eyes rolled back into his head. He clung to the bedpost. "Emily," he warned, even as his hips begin to thrust in time with her movements. "This isn't—I can't—get on the bed, Em. I need to be inside of you."

She knew that Cyrus was no virginal innocent, but he also wasn't a debauched rake and she took a measure of pride in driving him to the point where he lost all sense of propriety.

"You *are* inside of me," she said, swirling her tongue around the swollen tip of his cock and then sucking him in deeper.

She knew how to time the stroking of her hand on his shaft with the movements of her tongue and lips. She knew how to cup his stones and press down in the space right behind them. And if a gentleman so desired, she knew how to slick up a finger and press it into his ass to find that little spot that drove a man mad with passion. She could accomplish all of that in a matter of minutes and send the gentleman on his way, his step and his wallet lighter.

But she didn't want to suck Cyrus off and send him on his way. She didn't want this to be over in a matter of minutes. She wanted this to last the rest of their lives.

His shaft was slick with her spit as she licked and sucked and swirled her tongue around his cock. She could taste the salt of him dance over her tongue and he tasted so right that she almost cried with the joy of it all. And the whole time, she kept her gaze locked on his, watching him watch her.

God, she loved this. Men persisted with this notion that being sucked off somehow kept them in control of the sex when Emily knew that was only true if a woman felt shame at having a cock in her mouth.

Of course Emily didn't. She knew that she controlled everything about this. The sounds Cyrus made high in the back of his throat, the way his hips moved of their own accord. He was completely under her power right now. The thought made her pussy flood with wetness and she shifted, trying to relieve the pressure on her pearl. She desperately wanted him inside of her, too, but anticipation would drive both of their pleasure higher.

"Please, Emily," he begged, letting go of the bedpost to try and grab her under the arms.

Her mouth came off of him with a popping sound that made her grin. Slowly, she licked her lips, savoring every last drop of him. "Lay down on your back."

She didn't have to tell him twice. He shucked off his pants and shirt. She caught just a glimpse of his back. The scars still hit her like a punch, but she could see the gunshot wound was healing, smooth new skin growing where the ugly hole used to be. Then he was on the bed.

"Scoot toward the middle."

"You got something in mind?" His voice was a little more steady. She had stopped sucking him at just the right moment.

"I hope this isn't too scandalous for you," she murmured, undoing the rest of her buttons and shrugging out of her dress. She enjoyed fine dresses and, when they got to France, she would probably buy an entire new wardrobe from the very best modistes. But she couldn't understand why women insisted upon fashion that required one or even two additional people to get into and out of the dresses. Brevity and accessibility were the soul of wit.

"Have I told you that I love the fact that you don't wear any drawers?" Cyrus said as she sauntered to the side of the bed. "Every time I see you, the only thing I can think about is the fact that you're not wearing anything underneath that fine dress."

"Hmmm." She knew she was torturing him, but she couldn't help it. She licked the tip of her index finger and ran it down the center of his chest until she hit his cock. She brushed her fingernail over the opening at the tip and he moaned. "So responsive," she murmured. "I could spend the rest of my life making mad, passionate love to you and die a happy woman."

"I'm not going anywhere—not without you, that is," he added quickly when she paused. He held out a hand for her. "Come here, love."

"I'm not done sucking you," she informed him, kneeling onto the bed and swinging her leg over his waist. "But," she added, looking over her shoulder down at him, his eyes adorably wide with shock, "why should I have all the fun? Lick me, please."

156

She shifted back so that her pussy was close to his face and then gripped his cock again, stroking him slowly.

For a long moment, he didn't do or say anything. "Too scandalous for you?" she asked, kissing along the length of his shaft. Then she leaned down and ran her tongue along his stones.

He groaned but then, thankfully, he moved, his legs spreading to give her better access. "You—Jesus, Em." His hands skimmed up her bare thighs and wrapped around her legs, pulling her closer to his mouth. "You're so beautiful," he murmured. Then he touched her pussy, his fingertip sliding along her slit. "Look at you."

"Hmm," she said, letting the humming vibrations move from her mouth to his stone sac. His hips bucked in response.

"This isn't decent." But even as he said it, he pulled her thighs apart, spreading her wide for him.

"Decency is dull." She wet her fingertip and explored the space behind his stones while she sucked the tip of his cock back into her mouth.

"Holy..." then his mouth was upon her, a tentative kiss to the lips of her pussy.

She squirmed back against him, stretching out over his body, the tips of her nipples dragging over his stomach as she pushed herself up onto her elbows for better leverage.

She worked at his cock, but slowly. She knew he wouldn't last long, but that wasn't the point.

He'd found the solution. She wanted to reward him for that.

"This okay?" he asked. She couldn't see what he was doing but she could feel. He was licking at her pussy, one hand on her ass and the other spreading her pussy apart.

"It's wonderful, darling." Then he touched the bud of her asshole again. "Yes," she hissed, arching her back as she gripped his shaft harder. "Fill me up, Cyrus—in every way."

He growled, which sent vibrations skittering over the pearl of her sex and throughout her body. She could feel him spreading her juices over her bud, then his finger was inside of her ass and his mouth was on her pussy and she got so lost in the waves of pleasure that she lost the rhythm of sucking him off.

He was slow, thrusting his fingers into her ass. Her body tightened and loosened around his invasion, every spasm rocking her pussy. She couldn't control her reactions as Cyrus added his tongue to his kisses and then—

"Oh God, Cyrus," she gasped, throwing her head back as his teeth found her little pearl of pleasure and he sucked it into his mouth. A shiver ran over her entire body, a precursor to the orgasm that was building slowly but surely under his relentless touches.

"I'm going to do this to you every damn day," he growled, nipping at her. Then a second finger invaded her ass and she moaned in pleasure.

"Say it," she demanded, slicking up her finger and testing out his own bud. "Say what you're going to do to me, darling."

The tip of her finger disappeared into his body and he stilled.

"All right?"

"It's… yeah. It's different. Is this what it feels like for you?"

She laughed, raining kisses along his cock. "Having never been a man who's taken anything up the ass, I couldn't say. There's a little spot... ah," she said, working her finger into his body deeper and finding that pad of flesh. His body jerked under hers. "Yes, that," she said, satisfaction flooding her. "There's a spot men have right here." She stroked over that pad of flesh, watching his cock jerk and throb. "Good?"

She wanted it to be good for him. She wanted so much to enact all the perversions she'd discovered great joy in testing out over the years. She wanted to do everything naughty with him.

"Holy God," he got out in a ragged breath. "I... I had no idea."

She added more spit to her finger to keep things moving smoothly and then returned her attention to his cock. The head was swollen and she knew he was close to exploding in her face.

"I'm going to make you come now," she warned him, rotating her finger slightly as she licked a drop of his fluid off his tip.

"You... damn, woman!" he ground out, thrashing on the bed. His fingers left her body and his hands left her ass. He fisted the sheets. "You first."

"No, my darling. I insist." With that, she fell upon him, this time intent on her goal. She timed the thrust of her finger into his ass with the sucking of his cock. Her free hand held his shaft still so that she didn't break contact with him, squeezing in time.

It didn't take long before he began to spurt into her mouth. He cried out, grabbing her thighs and holding on as she greedily swallowed the torrents of his pleasure. When the rush was done, she eased her finger out of his body and went from sucking his cock to licking it.

His chest was heaving and she was impressed that she'd managed to stay astride of him, frankly.

"You didn't..." he panted as she patted his softening cock and looked at him over her shoulder.

"It's no great crime to come before me, Cyrus," she informed him as she rolled off to his side. "It's sweet of you to make sure I come first but I don't mind coming second."

"But I..." He waved at his spent cock.

She shot him a wicked grin and licked two clean fingers. Then, his gaze fastened on her fingers, she stroked them down her body and spread her pussy lips for him to see. "Perhaps you've realized there are other ways to bring me to crisis?"

Chapter Thirteen

If he were a younger man, Cyrus would be hard for her all over again. As it was, it felt like his heart was going to beat clean out of his chest. His own *crisis*, as Emily had put it, had left him sated and ready to sleep, but she was kneeling on the bed next to him, her knees spread wide so that she could stroke her pussy with her fingers. She cupped her breast with her other hand and teased her nipple and Cyrus wished mightily that he were a much younger man.

"You have something in mind?" He desperately wanted to get her off and then he wanted to pull her into his arms and never let go. He knew that wasn't an option—yet—but he could settle for satisfying her.

Still stroking herself, Emily leaned over and licked his own nipple. It sent a jolt through him and he gasped. She kept right on licking him, her tongue tracing a path over his chest to the hollow in his neck up to his ear. Then she straddled him and he moved toward her for a kiss, but she was in charge here. He loved her in charge.

Maybe it should bother him that even she didn't know how many men she'd slept with, but on the other hand, she knew things—things that he had no idea about. He never would've let anyone else put a finger into his ass, but he trusted her and when she had?

161

Jesus. He had never come so hard his entire life. She possessed a highly specialized, extensive knowledge and practical experience and he wasn't too proud to take advantage of that.

Like now. She scooted up over him, her knees above his arms and suddenly, he realized what she was doing. "You have the most marvelous mouth, Cyrus. Everything about you is marvelous," she added in an amused tone. "But I do so love your mouth."

He could smell her sex now—the sweet, salty cream scent filling his nose. She scooted forward a little more and all he would have to do would be to lift his head and he could taste her. He wrapped his arms around her thighs and pulled her forward that last few inches. "Does this mean you want to go to France?" he murmured against her inner thigh before pressing a kiss there.

"It is a brilliant idea, Cyrus." She shifted, drawing even closer. Then her weight settled and one of her hands dug into his hair. "Let me know any time if this doesn't work for you."

"It's working so far," he said, sticking out his tongue and slicking it over her sex.

"Yes, France," she said in an almost dreamy voice as he began to lick her in earnest. The folds of her flesh gave way beneath his tongue and his teeth. "Do you want to live in Paris or should we look for a small château in the countryside?" She began to rock her hips, gently at first but then with more energy. And she used the hand buried in his hair to guide him.

He surrendered himself to her, completely and totally. He ran his hands over her back and her bottom, stroking her but also digging his fingers into her flesh.

"Paris," he got out in between licks. "You belong in Paris."

"You may be correct." Her breath hitched as he hit that little button at the top of her sex. "But we should travel, also. A season in London—touring Italy—oh!"

"You going to talk this whole time?"

She looked down at him, so strong and proud and wicked and *his*. She was his. "Only until you make me stop talking."

"Woman," he growled and then he applied himself more fully.

"We'll hire the finest tutors for—oh, Cyrus," she gasped as he pulled her ass farther apart. Then he released those sweet cheeks and brought one hand down, a light swat. "Yes, that's good."

"Not good enough. You're still talking." He slipped his tongue inside of her pussy and then dragged it out up to that little button.

She tightened her grip on his hair, guiding his head to repeat that particular action again. Her weight settled down on him even more and her hips began to rock with more force now. Oh, yeah. He could make her stop talking.

He slapped her ass again and was rewarded with a little high-pitched noise that came deep from within her throat. "We should make Paris—oh, God—our home but let's see the—*oh*—world."

"Closer," he murmured, gripping her little button with his teeth and sucking on it.

Her hips bucked and he felt a spasm move through her body. That was the secret spot, apparently.

This was, by all reasonable measures, scandalous.

But he would be lying if he said that he hadn't ever thought of having Emily like this. Maybe he'd dreamed it, her sitting on his face like this, his tongue buried in her most private of places. She was shuddering and shaking above him, her hands guiding his head. She rocked on his body and even though he wasn't fucking her proper, he was still giving her what she needed and that made him feel damned good.

"What else do you want to see?" He asked not because he was paying attention to the answer but because he wanted to see if she could still form rational thought.

"Everything. Pyramids in Giza and India and—oh—I need—I need." Abruptly, she let go of him and shifted. She pitched one leg up so that her foot was on the bed, which put her pussy at an angle over Cyrus. But it also provided a little more room for him to work. Now, he could slip a hand up underneath her. "Suck my pearl while you put your fingers inside of me. *Please.*"

"So polite." Thankfully, the side she had opened up the space on was his good arm so he had no problems slipping it between her legs, finding her slit, and sliding two fingers into her. "Are you always this polite?"

She shook her head. "Many people want to be ordered about. I don't—you're not—oh, *God.* You're not like they are, Cyrus. I don't ever want to make you do something you don't want."

"I want to do this." With that, he gave up trying to make her talk and think and feel at the same time. He turned all of his attention toward making her shatter with pleasure. He nipped and sucked on that little button that she called her pearl and he worked

164

diligently to time his movements to the thrust of his fingers into her pussy.

With one hand, she held onto the headboard for balance but with the other, she grabbed hold of his hair again. He let her set the rhythm and then he realized, that with the angle his hand was buried in her body, he could also press his thumb against the little bud of her ass. So he did.

Her back arched and she cried out. Dimly, he thought that they would have to work harder on being quiet, especially if they were going to be in close quarters with Dolly, but right now, he couldn't care.

All he cared about was the way she kept saying, "oh—God, Cyrus. Oh. *Oh!*" As her hips ground down onto his face. Her sweet cream coated his mouth, his cheeks. All he could see, feel, smell and most definitely taste was Emily. She surrounded him. She was his whole world and as her body began to shudder with her crisis, he gave thanks to the merciful God that allowed them to find each other again.

She collapsed, falling off to the side of him. They lay there, a massive tangle of arms and legs, both breathing hard. He didn't want her to leave. He wanted her to stay right by his side. He knew she couldn't, but he wanted it all the same.

Long moments passed and he started to drift off to sleep when she stirred beside him. "So," she said, her voice shaky but sounding happy, "as you can see, I don't mind if you come first as long as you make sure that I come second."

He chuckled at that. "I'll remember." She stretched out alongside of him, curling into his side. "I wish you could stay."

"Soon," she promised. "Two weeks, maybe three. I have a lot of knots to untangle." She sounded sad about this and Cyrus felt the same way, but then she went on in a more businesslike tone, "Besides. You're still recovering. You need your rest."

He managed to notch an eyebrow at her. He would argue, except that he was having trouble staying awake. "Emily—in Paris—you won't whore, right?"

"Absolutely not." She sounded offended by this idea.

"And you won't run a brothel, right?" He knew he was risking her anger by asking but he didn't want there to be any misunderstandings between them.

"Cyrus, I'm going to retire," she said patiently. "The only person I want in my bed is you. I imagine that I'll have to find some cause to keep myself busy…"

He snorted. "I bet."

"But Mistress will not leave Brimstone. I will be a wife and mother."

That was a *yes* to his marriage proposal. His spirit soared and he hugged her to his chest. They'd have to get married sooner rather than later—otherwise, he'd go crazy thinking about it. "You'll come back to see me here, won't you?"

"Of course. But it won't be every day." With a sigh, she pushed her way out of bed and moved to the small washstand. She scrubbed up with a damp cloth, wiping her body clean. "It is a truly brilliant idea, Cyrus, but the plans have to be made to ensure your safety. And mine. You must give me time."

She was right. He wished she weren't, but she was. "Three weeks. And if you can't take the time to visit, could you at least send a note around every day? I don't like being in the dark."

She nodded and walked back to the bed, holding out her hand. He needed to get cleaned up but damn, it was tempting to pull her back down in bed and not let her out. He didn't. His heart was calming down now. The crisis, such as it was, had passed.

"Of course. You have your own plans to make, after all. But Cyrus?"

She was right. He had to talk to Isaac and get his cash. He found his feet and made sure he had his balance before he let go of her hand. "Yeah?"

She gave him a sly grin, the kind of grin that made him wonder what she was planning now. "We won't need your money."

Chapter Fourteen

As Mistress, Emily was used to commanding a room. Every flick of her wrist and flutter of her eyelashes communicated power and control.

So the fact that she was having trouble sitting still was unusual, to say the least.

France. Why hadn't she thought of it? It seemed so obvious in retrospect.

Of course, she didn't expect that Madame Colette's name carried any value in Paris. But that was fine. She didn't want to be Mistress anymore. If she were being honest, she hadn't wanted to be Mistress for a long while.

That was why, when Emmeline had married Raymond Dupree, Emily had felt so hurt. Emmeline had been her successor and suddenly, leaving the brothel behind became another problem that Emily didn't have a solution for.

Emily had so much to do. She kept a good portion of her fortune in the Brimstone bank, but she had hedged her bets against bank robbers and highwaymen. She had a few thousand here and a few thousand there and, like Cyrus, she had several thousand in New York. All told, she had well over half a million in relatively accessible cash, with more

168

invested in stocks, railways and mining operations. Her total worth was much closer to a million dollars.

More than enough money to arrive on the Paris scene and set herself up as an heiress, a woman so wealthy and powerful that she flouted social conventions and married whomever she loved.

Cyrus.

She wondered if this was what a phoenix felt like, because she was about to be reborn as Emily Franklin. The legend of Mistress would stay in Brimstone and Emily Weatherspoon had been gone for too many years to count.

She had been Emily Franklin when she had first fallen in love with Cyrus and now she could be that girl and that woman again.

There came a knock on her office door. "Come in."

The door creaked open and Beulah, looking worn and tired, poked her head in. "You asked to see me?"

"Yes, come in. Is Miss Ruby with you?"

Beulah swung the door open and Ruby entered the room behind her. "I'm here, Mistress."

Emily waited until the two women had closed the door and settled in the seats in front of her desk. "Beulah, you are more than welcome to stay here for as long as you'd like, provided that you earn your keep. Della says that you've been a great help in the kitchen."

Shakily, Beulah met her gaze. "That's a fine offer, ma'am."

Emily smiled gently. The poor woman had had a rough go of it and she was grateful for the offer, Emily could tell, but Beulah was not the kind of woman who belonged in a whorehouse. "However, I have a situation in…" She shifted the papers on the desk. "Ah, Yes. Louisville, Kentucky. An associate of mine could use a good cook." An old Jewel, so old, that Emily struggled to remember the woman's Jewel name because she had, for years, been Suzanne Van Haeckel, wife of Lionel Van Haeckel, a man who had made a fortune during the Civil War and now prospered buying and selling real estate around Kentucky. "It's with a husband and wife, with four beautiful children. They are a white family…" She always made sure to mention that, in case it was important, "but the position comes with room and board, Sundays off and a salary of twenty dollars a month. They're good people. They would not impose upon you and, should you decide to remarry in time, I'm sure that they would be happy to help you on your way."

During this recitation of facts, Beulah's eyes had grown wide and now they were suspiciously shiny. "You… you found me a position?"

Emily shrugged. She did this all the time, although very few people knew it. "They are friends and they sent word that if I knew anyone who would fit the requirements, to please send them along. If you're not interested in the position, I can—"

"I am," Beulah interrupted. "You say they're good people? Respectable Christian folk?"

"Methodist, I believe." She bit back a smile. Once, she had been a Baptist, but that had been a long time ago. "You did not think I would make you work on your back, did you?" she asked, knowing the answer.

"No, of course—no. I never," Beulah started babbling. "I appreciate everything you have done for me, ma'am. Seeing to Rob Boy, sheltering us and now this. Thank you. Thank you *so* much."

Emily turned her attention back to her papers. "There is a train that departs tomorrow morning at seven thirty. Here is your ticket and ten dollars traveling money. I'm sorry for the loss of your husband." She held out the papers.

But when Beulah rose to take them, Emily held fast. "There is a price for this, however." Beulah gasped. "The price is this. You are to act as another set of eyes and ears for the Mistress of the Jeweled Ladies. Should you ever hear of a girl being used wrong and there is no one else—the church, officers of the law, her family—who can help her out of her terrible situation, you are to send word here with what you know. And, on occasion, there may come a time when I ask for your help. There may be another woman who needs a position or perhaps even a new identity. You may be called upon to have a sister or shelter someone in some way. Can you do that?"

Beulah didn't debate for long. Nodding, she took her ticket and said, "I'll help Miss Della and then get my things packed."

Emily smiled, dismissing the woman. She hoped that Beulah's life would take a turn for the better from here on out.

Ruby came to her feet. She had followed the conversation closely, but wisely had chosen to remain quiet. "If you would stay, Ruby?" It was not a request.

With a look of confusion, Ruby resumed her seat. Neither of them said anything until the door shut behind Beulah. Then Ruby spoke. "Yes, Mistress?"

Emily kept her gaze focused on the papers on her desk. There is so much to do, but she really couldn't put off leaving. The longer Cyrus stayed in town, the

171

greater the risk and that was a risk Emily was no longer willing to take.

"I made an exception for you. You know that, don't you? Every other woman in this building came to me in a fashion similar to how Miss Beulah did. They were scared or wounded, so far down on their luck that they had forgotten what it looked like. You, Gertrude Kane, are the only woman I've ever said *yes* to who knocked on the front door of the Jeweled Ladies and requested employment—much less in a pair of men's trousers."

She glanced up to see Ruby watching her closely. "I needed a job."

Emily scoffed at this. "You're a nurse with battleground experience. You didn't *need* a job, Ruby. You *wanted* the work. I've never quite ascertained why you chose whoring over the more honorable profession of the medical arts but," she added, holding up her hand before Ruby could attempt to explain, "I suppose you're here for much the same reason the rest of us are. Money is power and this is one of the few places in this world where women such as us can have both at our beck and call."

Ruby exhaled a long, slow breath. It was her only reaction to the statement, but Emily had the suspicion that she had gotten close to the truth.

"I'm sure you've heard this from some of the other girls, but you were, in effect, a replacement for Miss Emerald Green. She is now Mrs. Emmeline Dupree, wife of the lieutenant governor of the state of Texas. I hired you because you had red hair and a willingness to work, and of course, your nursing skills have come in handy on several occasions. But I needed a redhead and you sufficed."

"Always pleased to have *sufficed,*" Ruby murmured under her breath.

Emily ignored this. "But perhaps you have not realized that, when Emmeline left, she did not just leave behind a life of whoring and coin. She left behind something more."

It was a long moment before Ruby finally broke and asked, "What was that?"

"The Jeweled Ladies. I had been training her as my successor so that I could one day retire. It was hers for the taking but the fool woman fell in love and got herself made into a proper woman." Emily shook her head, smiling at the memory of Emmeline's wedding. She had snuck into the church and hidden in the balcony. It simply would not have done to have the most notorious whore in Texas show up at a wedding, after all.

If possible, Ruby got even more still. "Why are you telling me this?"

"You know why. You sewed him up."

Ruby's eyes grew wide, and Emily thought, perhaps slightly afraid. "What are you saying?"

"I'm leaving," she said simply. "I tire of this life. I think I have been tired of it for a long time. And although I will not explain all of the details, suffice to say that Cyrus and I belong together and we always have. In a few weeks' time, we're going to leave this town and set sail for France. And, if she wants, we will take Dolly with us as our daughter."

Ruby blinked. "… And?"

"And I need a successor." Emily folded her hands together and looked hard at Ruby. "That would be you."

173

That was definitely fear dancing in Ruby's eyes, but there was something else there, too—excitement. That was when Emily exhaled in relief. She had made the right choice.

"You want *me* to have the Jeweled Ladies?" The color drained out of her cheeks. She looked like she'd been run over by a wagon.

"It seems a shame to shut it down."

"But I'm not... I don't have the skills to step into your shoes."

Emily waved this away. "I've spent years of my life building not only this brothel and a considerable fortune, but a network of informants among other madams and preachers, sinners and saints. Most women who come to me wind up like Beulah, washerwomen and cooks, teachers and even a few nurses. It's not just the brothel that I'm entrusting to your keeping, Gertrude. It is everything else. I could not have faith that Opal, bless her heart, would have the strength to rescue a girl being held as a sex slave. I do not believe that Garnet would be able to fire a weapon at a man threatening another's life. There is no way that Amber could stomach delivering a baby or sewing a man together. Amethyst would never be able to change her appearance and blend in with a rowdy saloon of men. Pearl would be incapable of taking orders and Beryl couldn't handle gentlemen callers who liked to give or receive pain or training girls to do one or the other. Each girl in this house has a talent and skill, but no one else has all of the skills necessary to continue the work that I have begun. Except for you."

"Except for me," Ruby said, her voice little more than a shaky whisper.

"And there is no one else but you to keep these secrets." Emily rose and moved to the wall of cabinets. "I have kept meticulous records over the years. Because a woman as intelligent as you knows that that's why they really pay us—to keep their secrets. You've shown me in the last few weeks that you alone are capable of wielding this much power and doing good with it. You may be a whore. I may be a whore. But that does not mean we cannot change the world for the better."

She would have to think of how she could keep doing her part while in France. Fund an orphanage, perhaps? Something. There was always misery that needed alleviating.

Ruby sat there, stunned. "I... This is all very sudden, Mistress."

"And for that, I am sorry. I had years of preparing Emmeline for this job and you, I am afraid, will get a week or two at most. But it can't be helped. Besides," she went on in a bright voice, "you'll do fine."

Ruby scowled at her, looking slightly more like her old self. "You're asking me for the impossible."

"Don't be dramatic. Nothing is impossible. This is merely improbable. I will leave you with a significant cushion of cash, although you should have no trouble lining your coffers. I believe I would like to make a grand exit," she mused. "Perhaps the town will even hold a parade in my honor, they'll be so glad to see me go."

Ruby laughed at that and Emily allowed herself to smile. "You will face opposition within the town," she went on. "Someone shot Cyrus and burned him out and there is undoubtedly a nefarious reason behind it.

But beyond that, I'm sure they hoped that, when I finally left, the Jeweled Ladies would curl up and blow away in the wind like a tumbleweed. But you can handle it." She hoped. "I believe a public announcement is the way to go. I'll need that young newspaperman. Mr. Thomas Haines, is it? Yes."

If Ruby couldn't handle the responsibility, the Jeweled Ladies would close. All good things must come to an end, after all, and as much as Emily wanted to see her legacy live on, she wouldn't look back. Lingering did no one any good.

"What do you say? Do you want it?" Any other time, those words uttered within this establishment would've had a completely different meaning.

Ruby considered. "Are Samuel and Della staying? I'll need help."

"That would be up to them. I wanted to approach you first. And if they choose to move on as well, there are other people who would come back." A thought occurred to her. "Perhaps even Cyrus's friend. He might need the work."

Ruby pushed to her feet, looking as if she suddenly had four hundred pounds of weight that she needed to shoulder. "This is insane. You know that, Mistress?"

She smiled warmly. A phoenix in the ashes—that was her. And she was just about to rise. "My name," she said, patting Ruby on the arm, "is Emily."

Chapter Fifteen

I'm leaving Brimstone," Cyrus announced into the silence of the kitchen.

Isaac notched an eyebrow at him and then motioned between the two of them.

Cyrus shrugged. "Don't rightly know if you'd want to come." He cared for Isaac a great deal. The man had gone from being a guest to a helper to a friend, but this was his new start with Emily and there was a small, selfish part of Cyrus that didn't want Isaac along. He'd spent years caring for others. He didn't want the additional burden of responsibility.

Isaac opened his hands and looked around.

"France," Cyrus said, answering the silent question. "Paris, most of the time."

All the blood drained out of Isaac's face and he slumped back in his chair.

Cyrus didn't know much about Isaac. Hell, he didn't even know the man's last name. But he'd shown up with a soiled dove that had been cut real bad and when the girl had died, Isaac had just stayed, silent and helpful. He must not have had anywhere else to go. And truthfully, Cyrus did feel badly about leaving him behind. But maybe it was best that Isaac move on. That dove, God rest her soul, had been buried for almost four years now.

"There's work for you at the Jeweled Ladies." That had been one of Emily's few messages to him. That his friend would have a job with Ruby, if he wanted. Isaac did not look mollified at this announcement. It hurt Cyrus to see him look so beat down but what could he do? "Do you want to go to France?" Just so there wasn't any confusion.

Isaac stared bleakly at the table and then shook his head no.

Cyrus didn't so much as exhale in relief. Not on the outside, anyway. "You'll be fine. Big, strong man like yourself? I'm sure that if you didn't want to work at the brothel, Mistress would know someone who'd need a hired hand."

He shrugged.

Just then, Hank O'Shea walked into the kitchen. "She's gone and done it now." He tossed the *Brimstone Gazette* onto the table in front of Cyrus.

"Done what?" Cyrus looked the paper over and saw immediately what, exactly, Emily had done.

"Mistress To Retire!" screamed the headline above the fold. "I shall miss the good people of Brimstone," read the sub heading.

"Oh, Lord," Cyrus muttered.

He skimmed the article. It was Emily in full-on Mistress mode. He smiled at the pack of lies she'd fed the reporter. She was retiring to San Francisco and looking forward to traveling by train on the newly completed Transcontinental Railroad through the mountains. "I've always wanted to see the mountains," the article quoted her as gushing. That was the word it actually used—"*she gushed.*"

There was to be a big send-off from the Jeweled

Ladies in two weeks' time. She'd hired a fine carriage to take her away and a private train car for the journey west.

That was laying it on a little thick, wasn't it?

The other interesting thing, buried deep in the article, was this—"However, Friends, do not despair. The Jeweled Ladies is not closing its doors. Instead, Mistress will hand the establishment over to the care of her favorite Jewel, Miss Ruby Red, who shall now be known as Lady Ruby. But when this humble reporter tried to ask Lady Ruby about how she was going to run the Jeweled Ladies, he was met with a cryptic smile and this quote: 'You'll just have to come see for yourself, won't you?' And indeed, that is a challenge many in this town will be happy to take up."

Isaac hit him in the arm, motioning for the paper.

Cyrus spun the newspaper so Isaac could read it and then turned his attention to Hank. "She seems to have her course set."

Emily was going to leave town in a fancy carriage, like a queen or something? He sighed. That woman may have talked a good talk about leaving Mistress behind but it wasn't going to be that easy.

Hank slid an envelope across the table. By now, Cyrus recognized Emily's stationary. He took it up and read it while Isaac read the newspaper.

"Darling, you've seen the paper by now, I trust. I have indeed hired a carriage and a private rail car. I shan't be getting on the train, though. I will switch to a different wagon at the station and then head south. I have contacted that Pinkerton agent, Mr. Shane, again. He is to join you and Dolly in a few days' time on your way to New Orleans. It would be best if you passed as a family and dressed Dolly as a boy. Once

179

there, arrangements have been made for your lodgings, and passage on a ship has been booked. We sail on the *Desdemona* for Calais on August 21st. I will be along shortly. Take care, my love."

Cyrus blinked at the letter, its full import becoming clear. She was, as always, running the world. And she meant to send him away without seeing him again.

Damn her hide.

A niggling lick of doubt crept up the back of his neck, that somehow this was all a ruse to get him out of town. She wasn't really going to give up her power and her wealth, certainly not for the likes of him. Who was he? Just a former slave, a man she claimed to love but had never once fought for. She'd married that preacher and refused to let Cyrus accompany them out west. She'd known he'd been in town for years but refused to acknowledge him.

All right, she'd saved him from being shot down in the street like a dog and nursed him back to health. She'd taken him to her bed, but she could have done that at any time in the last seven years. She hadn't had to wait until her only choices were saving his life or watching him die.

"You look a mite angry, friend," Hank casually observed, leaning back against the sink and sipping coffee. "Best coffee in Texas."

"Your coffee is crap," Cyrus said. He looked down at the note again. "I'm gonna guess that you know about this?"

"Afraid so. I send telegrams to Austin on a daily basis. It's not that unusual if I send more telegrams." Hank didn't even have the decency to look guilty about this. "Shane will be here tomorrow."

Cyrus rolled his eyes. "Is all this sneaking around really necessary?"

At that, Hank sobered. "Do not think for a moment that your absence hasn't been noted, my friend. I've got a few suspects in mind for who set you up but no one has confessed to anything definite. I'm confident that whoever she shot has left town because you're the only man with a hole in his shoulder I've come across, but that doesn't mean the walking wounded didn't have friends."

"Damn." For a ridiculous second, he just wanted things to go back to normal. But then he realized he was being an idiot because he actually didn't. Normal was living in his shotgun shack. Normal was wondering if the next person who came to his door was a traveler in need of help or an enemy looking to burn him out. Normal was being afraid to come into town for fear of being arrested and strung up. Normal meant Emily pretending he didn't exist because of some misguided notion that it kept him safe. He didn't want normal anymore, but he didn't know what his life would look like once he left this town.

He had no idea what to expect from France but it had to be better than here. Assuming, of course, that he made it to France with Emily.

"This isn't a trick, is it?" he asked Hank, motioning to the letter.

The Irishman stared at him. "Why would it be a trick?"

"That fool woman claims the reason she's kept away from me for the last seven years was to keep me safe." He was aware that Isaac was staring at him with renewed interest but he didn't care. "And before we

181

decided on France, she was going to send me and Dolly away to keep us safe. I just don't want this all to be a ruse to get me to leave her."

Hank stared at him for a moment before his face cracked into a smile. He reached into his coat pocket and pulled out a telegram. "If she's going to do that, she's playing a mighty deep game," he said, handing the telegram over. "Passage on a ship isn't cheap and she had me buy the most expensive cabins aboard the *Desdemona*. Three rooms. Two sleeping cabins and a sitting room."

Cyrus stared at the telegram. The berths were a hundred and forty dollars for two adults and eighty dollars for one child, which was a hell of a lot of money. He never had gotten Emily to admit to how much money she had, but maybe for the Mistress of the Jeweled Ladies, close to four hundred dollars was nothing. But surely Emily wouldn't spend that much on a ruse, would she?

"I'd be happier if we all went together," he grumbled.

"You think she'd jilt you like that?" Hank seemed genuinely incredulous at the mere suggestion. "Mistress always keeps her word."

"But Emily doesn't. Well, maybe she does. Hell, I don't know anymore." He dropped his head in his hands and stared at the papers spread out over the table. The newspaper interview, the letter and the telegram buying passage on the ships... he didn't like this crush of doubt and how it was playing tricks with his mind.

Dolly wandered into the kitchen, sleepily rubbing her eyes. She paused, looking at the three men with wide eyes. "What's wrong?"

"Nothing, hon," Cyrus said automatically, reaching out an arm to her and pulling her into a hug. "We're going to be leaving in a day or two. We'll go to New Orleans."

"Is she gonna meet us there? Or send us away? Because she said she was going to send me away." Dolly laid her head on his shoulder and something tightened in Cyrus's chest. Emily might try to pull a fast one over on him, but she wouldn't willfully hurt this child, would she?

Just last week, Emily had looked up at him with her big eyes and asked if he thought Dolly looked like her sisters. Cyrus's memories of Emily's sisters were hazy. They'd always been in the big house instead of working in the fields, personal servants to their half-sister. They'd been quiet girls, smiling softly whenever they ventured out of the house with Emily to visit the slaves' shacks, but always with extra food and books in their pockets, maybe soap or whatever else the three girls had decided to steal. Emily had always been the leader, of course, with Liza, the older of the two, following close along and Junie, the baby, dragged behind them.

When Chester Franklin had sold the girls away just like *that*, it was as close to breaking as he'd ever seen Emily. In all honesty, that was as near as Cyrus could figure as to why Chester had had him whipped to within an inch of his life. The master hadn't been trying to punish Cyrus for any real or imagined transgressions, but he'd been trying to break Emily's spirit. The old man hadn't been stupid, just cruel, and he must have figured that, by selling Liza and Junie and then beating Cyrus almost to death, he'd put his daughter in her proper place without ever laying a hand on her.

That man had never known the true strength of Emily and he'd vastly underestimated Cyrus's will to live. In the end, Emily had put her father in *his* place, in an unmarked grave outside the family cemetery, destined to be forgotten. Not like Junie and Liza.

Mistress wouldn't have kept the girl. She would have shipped Dolly out the next day, if not sooner, to a safer place. But Emily? Emily had risked everything to take this girl in and keep her close. Because Dolly was the daughter they'd never had.

"She's going to meet us there, hon," he said, putting more conviction into his words than he felt.

"Promise?"

"Promise," Cyrus agreed. He leaned back and looked down at Dolly. Yes, he could see a resemblance to those girls, lost so long ago. "We'll be a family from here on out, if that's okay with you."

Her eyes got real wide. "Really? I never had a pa before," she added, looking ashamed of that fact. "No one ever claimed me before."

"Well, I'm claiming you. It'll be a mighty big change, moving to another country, but I'll be your father and she'll be your mother and we'll be together, always."

God, he hoped he was telling the truth.

Dolly threw her arms around his neck and hugged him real tight. "Oh, thank you! Thank you!"

His eyes watered as he hugged her back. "We gotta hide just a bit longer, hon. And we're going to have to dress you up as a boy, okay? But then we'll get on a big ship and everything will be just fine."

And that *would* be the truth, if he had anything to say about it.

Chapter Sixteen

Emily had anticipated that business would pick up after her newspaper interview, but not even she had predicted the level of interest. Men were traveling from miles around to offer her truly insane amounts of money for one night with Mistress. Why, cattle baron Boyd Brennan had ridden all the way up from El Paso to offer her one thousand dollars for two hours of her time. It was almost enough to make an old whore weak in the knees.

Almost. But not quite.

Most of the callers settled for a preview, such as it was, with Lady Ruby at double her normal rates.

Mistress swanned around the parlor and the saloon, both of which were twice as crowded as normal, speaking with everyone who wanted a moment of her time. She kept her smile bright and her eyes excited, spinning fantastical tales about the life she planned to lead in San Francisco.

Yes, she'd already rented the house.

No, she would not be entertaining gentlemen callers there. The local madams might not appreciate her moving in on their territory.

Indeed, she repeated more times than she could count, she was looking forward to a nice, quiet retirement. She always said it with a hint of humor in her voice and everyone laughed, as if they all knew that Mistress could never truly live a quiet life.

It wasn't just the men who came, either. The brothel no longer opened at four, but at one in the afternoon so that those who were less interested in vice could stop by without it being quite as unseemly.

Her most notable guests arrived to much fanfare. Emmeline Dupree waltzed into the brothel on the arm of Lt. Gov. Raymond Dupree. The two of them took up residence in one corner of the parlor and were almost as mobbed as Emily was. After all, it wasn't every day that the lieutenant governor stopped by to visit. Sadie and Gerard Hobson, special counsel to the governor of Texas, also made the trip down from Austin and the fact that one of her staunchest enemies was willing to be seen in the brothel was akin to opening the floodgates.

Suddenly, it was acceptable for men and their wives to stop by on their way to somewhere else. Of course, Emily knew most of the women personally. They had either come by themselves or with their husbands, for whatever reason. But they never would have otherwise shown their face anywhere near the Jeweled Ladies and certainly not when other people could witness them doing so.

Aside from the gratification of having so many men offer so much money for one last night with her, these visits put a smile on her face. For every fool who wanted to be parted from his money, another man or woman would pull Emily aside and quietly whisper their thanks. Men who had been terrified of their desires, women who had been slowly dying inside from the lack of passion, even a few women whom she had helped get pregnant when their husbands were unable or unwilling to perform. All of those people had considered their secrets shameful, and therefore, had nowhere else to turn but to the one woman in Brimstone without shame—Mistress of the Jeweled Ladies.

And then there were the former Jewels. Married women, businesswomen, almost two dozen of her girls came back to send her off. Jewels that had married farmers and cowboys made the trip into town. Emily managed to spend some time in private with each of her former girls and her current ones, although that was easier to pull off. Everyone wanted to know about her new life in San Francisco and Emily felt bad about lying to her girls. Once a few months had passed, she decided, she would send word back that San Francisco hadn't suited her and she had decamped to Paris. By then it should be safe. In the meantime, she turned the attention back onto her former Jewels, smiling at each detail of their new lives as respectable wives, mothers and businesswomen. And from those who couldn't come for farewell in person, telegrams and letters came pouring in. A pair of gloves arrived, hand sewn by Abigail White, with a note from Minerva Krenshaw tucked inside the left glove, thanking Emily profusely for helping Minerva and Abigail find each other.

Yes, it was all very gratifying. Emily had done much good in the world during her years as Mistress. She had seen problems and solved them—perhaps not how everyone else would've solved them, but wasn't that the point? Yes, it had made her rich, but in her own way, she had been selfless.

All right, that might be a bit of a stretch but she had earned her retirement. She had earned this space to be just a little bit selfish with Cyrus.

Finally, the day arrived. Trunk after trunk was loaded onto separate carts and sent ahead to the train station. Most of the trunks were empty or filled with random rags to give them weight.

Contrary to appearances, Emily was traveling light. She had three small trunks that were going to go on the carriage with her. She was only taking enough dresses to get her through the sea voyage and those first weeks in Paris. Beyond that, she had a few mementos that she wanted to keep.

Her wedding ring had been sold for cash decades ago, but she still had Phineas Weatherspoon's Bible. Perhaps it was sacrilegious to pack that next to her carved wooden phallus, but Emily was nothing if not sacrilegious. She sewed her many gems into the petticoats of her dresses and withdrew as much money as she could safely carry. Everything else would be transferred to the bank in New York and from there, to a bank in Paris.

All that was left to do was wait.

Emily hated waiting. Normally, she could be quite patient when it came to dealing with someone else's problems and solutions, but it had already been two and a half weeks since she had last seen Cyrus. She knew that they had made it to New Orleans—Mr. Shane had telegrammed Hank O'Shea to that effect. She shouldn't be worried about him or Dolly, but she was.

Oh, if only she knew who had set the trap for Cyrus. She'd feel better with those people dead or, at the very least, locked up. But she didn't and Hank had not been able to find out anything one way or the other. As such, with the would-be murderers on the loose, Emily couldn't relax until they were off this continent.

"Are you going to make it?" Hank asked, his voice low in her ear. She had chosen him as her guest to accompany her out of town. Over half the town was convinced that their relationship went beyond that of client and madam. Hank had stuck close by her over the last few weeks and she found reassurance in his presence. There was no confusion about the nature of their relationship. Hank was committed to the Duprees and Emily was committed to Cyrus, but they both knew how to put on a good act and appearances were what mattered.

"Of course," she said, adding a coquettish laugh and swatting at his arm. "How much longer until the carriage gets here?" The wait was interminable.

Hank slipped his arm around her waist and pulled her against his broad chest. They were alone in the parlor of the Jeweled Ladies. Everyone else was outside—even Della and Samuel. Leaving them was harder than Emily had expected it to be. As anticipated, neither of them particularly wanted to uproot their lives. They were happy to stay on and guide Ruby through the finer points of brothel ownership and management. But this morning, Della had thrown her big arms around Emily and cried. In all of the years that they had been together, Emily had never seen the woman cry. Even Samuel had gotten misty-eyed. Which of course made Emily weep and it all went downhill from there until Della had straightened and scolded Emily to knock off this foolishness, they all had work to do. Emily would miss them dearly. They had been together for over fifteen years. It truly was the end of an era.

"Here it comes," Hank whispered in her ear. And indeed, a glorious carriage rounded the corner and came to a halt in front of the Jeweled Ladies. A cheer went up. The carriage was surrounded by four outriders, Pinkerton agents armed to the teeth.

A tall, thin man hopped down from the driver's box and came around to open the door of the carriage. The crowd quieted as everyone waited for Emily to make her appearance.

"It's time," Hank said. "Ready?"

Emily stepped back and took one last look at her brothel, her home for the last twelve years. "I've never been more ready."

She exited the Jeweled Ladies on Hank's arm, beaming and waving as another cheer went up. Hank handed her up into the carriage and followed suit. The man climbed in after them and shut the door. Then they were off.

Emily waved out the windows at all of the well-wishers. It seemed the whole town of Brimstone had turned out for this. Whether they were glad to see her go or crushed by the loss, not a single soul in town was willing to miss this. They drove past Snyder's dry-goods store, where Mrs. Snyder was dabbing at her eyes, no doubt crestfallen that her best customer was leaving town. School children ran behind the carriage and Hank threw out a handful of coins for them to pick up.

The train station had been built just north of town—a ten-minute walk on a good day. Today, however, the trip was planned to take close to twenty minutes. The carriage moved at a sedate pace, careful not to trample any of the crowd.

Emily turned to the 'man' sitting next to her.

Ruby had already removed her hat and bandana and was undoing the buttons on her men's shirt. "Ready?"

"No peeking," Ruby said to Hank as she skinned off her clothes.

Hank scoffed at this. "Who do you think is going to help with your buttons?"

They worked quickly. Underneath her clothes, Emily was wearing a pair of men's trousers. She stripped off her dress and handed it over to Ruby, who passed the men's shirt back to Emily. Hank did indeed do up Ruby's buttons while Emily shoved her feet into men's boots.

Unlike Ruby, Emily felt odd in all of this clothing, but appearances were everything and as far as anyone else would see, Mistress would indeed get aboard the train steaming toward San Francisco.

"I'm looking forward to some quiet time in my own private car," Ruby said, lifting her hips so the dress's skirts could be swept under her legs. "After the last few weeks? I could use a nap."

"Will you be all right?" That was another concern that Emily had not had much time to fret over. Yes, she had faith that Ruby would make a fine madam, but there hadn't been time for anything other than the most basic overview of what Emily did on a day-to-day basis that went above and beyond peddling flesh.

Emily unpinned her hat and scraped her hair up into a rough knot on the top of her head. Then she crammed Ruby's hat down over it while Ruby pinned Emily's hat over her own red hair.

"It'll be fine," Ruby said, sounding like she was trying to convince herself as well as Emily. "I don't want you to worry."

Emily would, of course. Whoever had attempted to murder Cyrus was still out there and her leaving wouldn't end the risks to the Jeweled Ladies or the girls who came through its doors. But those problems were no longer her main concern. She had a boat to catch.

They arrived at the station. Emily opened the door and hopped down. Hank climbed out and then handed out Ruby, now bearing a vague resemblance to Mistress. With a farewell wink, Hank escorted Ruby to the private car Emily had hired and that was that.

The station was crowded and Emily was afraid someone would realize that it was not her getting into the train car. After all, Ruby was taller and thinner that Emily was. But no one amongst the well-wishers seemed to notice. They saw Mistress's dress and Mistress's hat and the man Mistress had been keeping company with over the last month and that was good enough for them.

No porters came to unpack the small trunks tied to the top of the carriage. Emily climbed up into the driver's box and sat next to the Pinkerton agent who had a shotgun across his lap. "Ready?"

She glanced back over her shoulder. She could see Ruby at the window. She waved and Ruby waved back.

Then Emily faced forward. Lingering never did anyone any good and Cyrus was waiting for her. "Let's go."

Chapter Seventeen

It turned out there wasn't much Emily hadn't thought of.

"Mr. Franklin?"

Barely at the top of the gangplank, Cyrus looked in the direction of the voice and saw a tiny white woman dressed in demure shades of dark blue. She didn't look like the rest of the crew aboard the *Desdemona*. "Yes?"

"I am Mrs. Basil T. Farnsworth," she announced, giving a curtsy that made her look like a doll come to life. "I am to be Miss Franklin's nanny and governess." She turned her attention to Dolly and smiled. "Hello, dear."

"Ma'am," Dolly said, clinging to Cyrus's side. At least she was back in a dress today.

Mrs. Farnsworth took one look at the sad state of Dolly's hair and sighed heavily, as if she knew she had much work to do. Then she turned her attention back to Cyrus. "I am a respectable widow, Mr. Franklin," she said, straightening. Really, she was so small that she had barely two inches on the girl. "Some years ago, Mistress saved me from a fate worse than death, of that I have no doubt. Thanks to her, I have been a governess in Atlanta for the last six years. It is an honor to accompany you on this voyage and help prepare Miss Franklin for her new place in society as the daughter of an heiress."

Cyrus knew that rich people hired tutors and governesses for their children all the time, but it made him uneasy. He and Dolly had gone along just fine over the past few weeks. Emily had gotten them room and board in one of the nicer boarding houses that catered to black folks. They'd worked on reading but they'd also taken time to walk through New Orleans, listening to the music and eating the food. It'd been a kind of freedom he hadn't felt in a while. Freedom that came with being just another face in the crowd, instead of having to worry that someone had it out for him.

He'd kept Dolly dressed as a boy while they'd wandered because he'd thought that would make them less noteworthy. Despite the clothes, every time he looked at her, he saw Emily. Oh, he knew damned well there was no blood relation, but Dolly was Emily's daughter by choice. Dolly was *his* daughter by choice and he wasn't going to let the girl go anytime soon, no matter where they wound up. But he would feel so much better if Emily were here. He didn't want to doubt her, but he couldn't help himself.

Still, Mrs. Farnsworth was right about something. Cyrus may be able to take care of Dolly just fine when she was pretending to be a boy, but he had no idea what things the girl would need to know in Paris. Hell, he didn't know all the things Emily probably took for granted, such as which knife and fork to use, how to address royalty or even servants. He'd never had servants. He'd made his own coffee, cooked his own food, made his own bed. How was he going to fit into her world?

"Why, that'd be real good," he said, because at the very least, Mrs. Farnsworth would be a good teacher for Dolly.

"Miss Franklin, I have a lovely book of fairy tales. Perhaps we can work on reading it together after we tour the ship?" Mrs. Farnsworth had a gentle manner about her, but for all of her tininess, she still carried a measure of authority in her voice. "I believe the ship's cook has some fresh-baked cookies, just out of the oven."

Dolly looked up at Cyrus. "Is that all right, Papa?" She'd been calling him that since they'd left Brimstone.

And, just like every other time she said that word, Cyrus's heart tightened with joy. No, he wasn't going anywhere without his daughter. "Sure is, hon. Mind Mrs. Farnsworth and I'll come get you when your mother gets here."

But the word felt strange in his mouth. What was he to call Emily? He couldn't still call her Mistress and Mother still felt wrong. And, as they weren't married yet, he couldn't very well call her his wife, either.

If they could have gotten married before he'd left Texas behind… it would have ruined the plan but *still*. A marriage would've been hard proof of her commitment to him.

As Dolly and Mrs. Farnsworth went off together, all he could think about was the time Emily had called him into her father's office in the big house—when he'd been last to receive his freedom. How he'd thought they were going to be together for the rest of their lives but instead she'd sent him away. There were differences, sure, and more than just the number of years that had passed. Back then, she'd never promised to take him with her. He'd just assumed that they'd be together. This time, she had said she would meet him at the ship. They had made plans.

He leaned out over the railing, his gaze fastened to the dock below. If she didn't show up before the ship set sail, he'd get off this ship. Mrs. Farnsworth and Dolly would come with him. One thing was for certain, he wasn't leaving without Emily and that was final.

The dock was busy. Cotton and tobacco were being loaded into the hull of the ship. Not so long ago, all of that would've been picked by slaves. Cyrus would have picked some of that cotton himself, day after backbreaking day in the baking Georgia sun. He had held a great many jobs after he had walked away from the Franklin plantation. He'd worked on docks, driven supply wagons in the Civil War, shoveled coal, but he had never worked the fields again.

It wasn't such a bad thing, leaving this place behind. He'd been born in America and so had his mother. His father? He didn't know. But this country had never really felt like home to him. This country was for other people who had built their homes upon his back. If he ever set foot in America again, he hoped like hell it would be a better place.

A sailor in a crisp naval jacket came to Cyrus's side, watch in hand. "Mr. Franklin," he began, his voice resonant. "I'm Captain Bedford, pleased to welcome you aboard the *Desdemona*. Should you or your traveling companions require anything, please don't hesitate to ask."

Cyrus shot an amused look at the man. This was something he needed to get used to—people treating him so respectfully. Who would have ever thought it? "Captain Bedford, it's a pleasure."

"Would you like to see your cabins?"

Cyrus shook his head. "I'd rather wait for my— for Emily."

The Captain looked at his watch again. "We're pushing the tides. But," he added, before Cyrus could do something uncalled for, like demand this ship wasn't going anywhere without Emily, "we're not to leave without her, rest assured."

The Captain's skin was dark, but Cyrus couldn't tell if that was because he had African blood or he'd lived his life in the sun. Either way, he didn't look at Cyrus as if he were a piece of property too disgusting to name and for that alone, Cyrus was grateful.

"You often hold for a tardy passenger?"

The Captain smiled, looking sharp. "Never. But then, most passengers do not pay for the privilege. Tides come and go, Mr. Franklin. But well-indulged passengers are as rare as a blue moon." He gave a salute as crisp as his jacket and turned to go.

"Captain Bedford?" When the man turned back to Cyrus, he asked the question that had been on his mind for weeks now. "You marry people at sea, don't you?"

"That I do." He waggled his eyebrows. "With fair winds, we'll sight France in five weeks. A man can have a lot of fun in that amount of time."

Cyrus must've looked offended, because the Captain slapped him on the back, laughing loudly. "Easy, man. We so rarely get newlyweds aboard this ship. And see? She's here now. Saved you all that worry." He began to whistle a jaunty tune and strode off, yelling orders at his crew.

Captain Bedford was right. A cart had pulled up, three small trunks in the back and there, in the driver's box, was Emily. She was wearing a dress that Mistress never would've been caught dead in—a simple, understated, plain light blue cotton with a white shawl. She tilted her head back and looked up at the ship underneath the brim of her straw bonnet and when she saw Cyrus, she broke into a wide smile.

The relief was so intense that his knees almost buckled. He shouldn't have doubted her. He never would again. Because she'd done it. She'd given up her power and—well, maybe she hadn't given up her wealth, but she had given up her work, which was the key to even more wealth. She had sacrificed Mistress to be with him.

His vision blurred as she climbed down from the cart. The Captain himself rushed down to escort her up the gangplank and by the time Cyrus's vision cleared, she was making her way toward him.

He tried to speak, but nothing came out. All he could do was stare at her and swallow as he tried to move past the lump in his throat.

"Oh, ye of little faith," she teased, but her eyes were bright as he took her hands and pulled her close. He didn't embrace her, not yet—they weren't out to sea yet.

Around them, final preparations were being made. Captain Bedford was yelling at his first mate, the first mate was bellowing at the crew, but it all was just noise. "I'm supposed to tell Dolly when you get here," he said dumbly.

"Is Mrs. Farnsworth with her?" Cyrus nodded. "In a moment, then."

The Captain reappeared at their side. "Your berths, ma'am?"

"Of course." Even as Emily, she still commanded the respect and attention of every single person on this ship. Heads turned and grizzled old sailors whipped off their hats as she passed.

They followed Captain Bedford to their cabins, but Cyrus hardly noticed anything about the small rooms, save the bed bolted to the floor. "Another hour before we'll be safely out of port," the Captain said, closing the door behind him. "I'll let young Miss Franklin steer the ship in the meantime, shall I?"

"Yeah," Cyrus said, not really hearing the words. He was aware when the door shut and then Emily was in his arms. "Babe," he groaned, lowering his mouth to hers.

"I missed you so much, my darling." Her mouth traced a trail from his lips over his jaw and down his neck.

His pulse jumped up as his body strained for hers. He wasn't sure he'd ever been this hard before. "Marry me," he begged, bending down to lift her skirts. "Marry me today. This evening. As soon as we've made open water."

"Yes," she gasped as his hands traced her calves and he pushed her skirts up higher. "Oh, God—yes, Cyrus."

No drawers. His cock jumped when he hit her creamy thighs, not a stitch of cotton between her pussy and his touch.

"You didn't think I'd suddenly get all

199

respectable, did you?" she laughed, swaying her hips as she backed up toward the bed. "I will always be scandalous for you, Cyrus. Oh my darling, you have no idea how very scandalous I can be."

"Yeah," he said, giving himself over to the lust. She was here, she was his and by God, he was going to have her. Not just right now, not just tonight, but for the rest of his life.

He turned her around and bent her over the edge of the bed. A mirror nailed to the wall over the washstand caught them in action as he exposed her beautiful ass. "Stay scandalous, Emily. But just for me. Only for me."

"Only for you," she agreed, spreading her legs and bracing herself. She caught sight of the mirror and sighed, a happy sound. "I'm waiting on you, Cyrus."

"Woman," he growled. "Been waiting on you for weeks. Was afraid you wouldn't come." He fumbled out of his pants, watching his reflection in the mirror as he fit the head of his cock to the entrance of her pussy. With a wild thrust, he buried himself in her. The sensations almost overwhelmed him and for a long moment, he couldn't do a thing but stand there. Then he gripped her ass and began to thrust, watching how his body slid into and out of hers in the mirror. "Don't ever leave me waiting again, Emily."

"Never. Oh—Cyrus!" She writhed underneath him, lifting her ass so he could hit that spot of hers. Which he must have done because she grabbed a pillow off the bed and cried into it, the sound muffled. "Harder. Fuck me harder—*yes*!"

Later, there'd be time to make love to her, but right now, Cyrus just wanted to give her what she wanted. He wanted to punish her for staying away from him and he wanted to love her for coming to him, and more than anything else, he wanted to claim her as his and be claimed in turn.

He was on a ship, sailing into the unknown, but Emily was with him, finally and forever.

This was his home.

He slammed into her, pushing her pleasure higher as he dug his fingers into her pale flesh. His climax roared through him and he watched the whole thing in the mirror. Emily's back arched and she screamed into the pillow. God, he'd never seen anything so beautiful, so raw.

He withdrew and sank down next to her. For some reason, she was laughing and he was laughing with her.

She reached over and stroked his cheek. "There you are," she said tenderly and the love he had for her in his heart swelled. "*Now* we can get married."

And that was exactly what they did.

Epilogue

S weetheart," Cyrus said, coming to his feet and catching her in his arms, "you're going to wear a hole in the rug."

Emily leaned into him, but without taking her eyes from the front window. "I can buy new rugs," she murmured, settling into his grasp. "But I only have two sisters."

"They'll get here when they get here," he said, his voice low and close to her ear. "It's a long trip from Canada."

"They should have been here hours ago." She knew she was being ridiculous but she was unable to help it. If she'd had her way, she would have magically whisked Junie and Liza here the moment she'd gotten the telegram from Mr. Shane, informing her that, after all these years, he'd located a pair of half-black sisters in Toronto who had a powerful reaction to the name Emily Franklin.

In the weeks that had followed, Emily had all but lost the ability to sleep, to eat—to do anything but bring her sisters to her. She had almost hightailed it to Canada herself, but Cyrus had reasoned that it was best to wait and see what Junie and Liza wanted to do.

202

More telegrams had gone flying back and forth across the ocean before Emily had arranged for passage for Junie, Liza and Junie's husband, a freeman named Tom Coleman and their children, to make the trip across the pond.

They were supposed to arrive today. Emily was going out of her mind with worry.

"Mama," Dolly said, setting aside her embroidery and moving to the piano, "shall I play you a song?"

"Yes, dear. That would be lovely," Emily said, knowing full well that Dolly's playing would not get her sisters here any faster. But their daughter had a beautiful singing voice and had taken to the piano like a duck to water. Her musical talent was known throughout the salons of Paris. Mme. Emma Calvé herself had taken note of Dolly's gifts and had expressed interest in making Dolly her protégée.

Dolly played something soothing and quiet, a composition of her own that Emily recognized.

"Soon, babe," Cyrus whispered in her ear and she sighed in satisfaction.

God, she loved this man. The last six years had been nigh-onto heavenly.

Although it was not fashionable, she and Cyrus shared a bedroom. He was slowing down as he got closer to sixty—and she was no spring chicken herself—but they still spent long mornings in bed, satisfying their needs. His shoulder ached when it rained, so they had taken to traveling during the worst of the winters, exploring the warmer climates of Spain and Italy and Greece.

Dolly's education had been quite thorough in no small part to their travels. Mrs. Farnsworth had stayed with them for years. Despite her late start with reading, Dolly had picked up written English and then, seemingly overnight, absorbed French and had recently begun to learn Italian, just in case she had a career in the opera ahead of her. Now seventeen, she was every bit as beautiful as Emily had predicted. Dolly was taller than Emily and Cyrus, but her figure had blossomed into the first flush of early womanhood and, after much trial and error, they had finally found a maid who could tame her hair into ringlets.

To think Emily had almost sent the girl away. It would have been the second greatest mistake of her life, right after sending Cyrus away when she'd sold the plantation.

They had settled into a fashionable *plaine Monceau* neighborhood in Paris and Emily had done what she did best—become a vital social center amongst the ton.

With one major difference, of course. No one in this house whored.

"We cancelled the salon, right?" she asked, knowing they had but unable to keep from fretting. Every Wednesday night, she and Cyrus hosted the premiere salon of Paris, where expatriates and starving artists mixed with the cream of the Parisian society.

One thing had not changed—Emily couldn't help but accumulate secrets.

Heavens only knew how many men and women she had paired up—plain heiresses with a need to dominate with cash-poor barons who liked a woman with a whip, starving male sculptors with lonely older noblemen, dissatisfied couples with the young man or woman who brought the spark back to their marriage, women who had been seduced and abandoned with men who didn't care about hymens. She couldn't help it. Apparently, something about her being an American married to a black man meant people trusted her. Or perhaps that was just the lingering vestiges of her Mistress charms. Either way, after strong French wine, she often found herself pulled into a small parlor, some poor soul sobbing on her expensive silk dresses as they poured out their hearts.

People brought her their problems. And if there was one thing Emily was good at, it was solving problems. The more problems she solved, the greater her reputation became.

She leaned forward, following the path of a carriage on the street. It did not turn into the courtyard and she stamped her foot in frustration. Her sisters were a problem she had been trying to solve for years and finally, the solution was near.

"What if they hate me?" she heard herself murmur to Cyrus. It was possible. She had no notion of their lives after they'd been sold by their father.

"I doubt they'd sail halfway around the world if they hated you," her husband replied with a chuckle.

Another carriage appeared on the street and turned into the courtyard. "It's them!"

She pulled free of Cyrus's arms as Dolly's song came to an abrupt halt. Normally, Emily would await her guests in the Blue Salon or, if she were comfortable with them, she might even receive them in her private sitting room, like she had with the Duprees and Hank O'Shea on their family trip to Paris three years ago.

But for this momentous occasion, she rushed to

the front door and threw it open herself before the butler could take command of his post, impropriety be damned. She simply couldn't wait another second.

She was halfway down the stairs when the footman opened the carriage door. A tall gentleman in a black suit, his skin the color of mahogany, emerged first. This must be Tom Coleman. He looked at Emily and then Cyrus as he came to stand next to her on the steps before nodding. Then he turned back to the carriage and handed out—

"Junie," Emily breathed as her sister emerged. She was so much taller than Emily expected, but then again, she'd been sold away when she'd been little more than nine.

She all but flew down the stairs and then her arms were around Junie and Junie was hugging her back and they were laughing and crying all at once.

"You grew up!" Emily gasped. "You're beautiful!"

"So did you," Junie replied, pushing back to stare down at Emily. "You are quite the grand lady, aren't you? How did this all come about—Oh! Cyrus!"

"Miss Junie," Cyrus said, bowing over her hand. "Been a long time, but I'm mighty glad you made it here."

Tom Coleman harrumphed impressively, looking dignified and yet still put-out.

"Wait," Emily said, wiping her tears. "Liza?"

"The journey was harder on her," Junie warned.

"Don't be talking like that," a voice echoed from the carriage. "I'm not dead!"

Emily began to laugh again, just to hear Liza's voice. Yes, it was crackled with age, but she'd know that voice anywhere. "Then come out here and prove it!"

Together, she and Junie held out their hands for Liza. The years had not been as kind to Liza, who was three years Junie's elder. Liza was bent over and used a cane to balance herself as she stepped down. One of her eyes was milky white, but she straightened, coming to Junie's shoulder and nearly a height with Emily. "Not deaf, either."

Once her feet were firmly on the ground, Emily threw her arms around Liza and squeezed tight. "My sweet Liza," she murmured. Liza was only two years younger than Emily and had always been her closest confidant. "Oh, how I've missed you."

"Never thought I'd live to see the day," Liza replied, her voice muffled against Emily's shoulder. "But I sure am glad I did."

Two handsome young people emerged next— Junie's children. Emily's heart clenched so hard her eyes started to water again. "Oh, my goodness," Emily breathed. These were her flesh and blood, her niece and nephew. She was an aunt.

For so long, she'd separated herself from the Franklin family name. Her father's brother had died years ago and Emily had not sought out any of her cousins on either side of her family tree. Chester Franklin and everything he stood for was dead. Except for her and Junie and Liza. Except for Junie's children. There had been very little good in Chester Franklin but the best of him now stood before Emily, proud and unbroken. Even Liza, who'd clearly had a harder life, stood straight, looking at her niece and nephew with obvious pleasure.

Junie beamed. "Emily, Mr. Franklin, may I present my husband, Dr. Tom Coleman and my children, Adam and Evangeline? Tom, this is my sister, Emily Franklin and her husband, Cyrus."

Emily knew she shouldn't but she cupped Evangeline's face. The young woman was in her early twenties, perhaps—older than Dolly, but not by much. "You look so like your mother," she said before hugging the girl. Then she turned her attention to Adam, as handsome a young man as she'd ever seen. But he wasn't paying any attention to her or, indeed, anyone else clustered around the carriage. Instead, his gaze was locked on the top of the steps.

Emily followed his eyes and there stood Dolly, the late dusk sunlight setting a golden glow around her. She looked like an angel come to earth to bless this family in their reunion.

The look Adam was giving Dolly heated the air.

"Ah," Emily said, smiling knowingly. She might not know Adam Coleman but oh, how she recognized the look on his face. "May I present Miss Dorothea Franklin, our adopted daughter?" Because of the way Adam was gaping, Emily felt it important to highlight that he was in no way a blood relation of Dolly's.

"Miss Franklin," Adam said, stepping around his parents and executing a lovely bow at Dolly's feet. "It is an honor to make your acquaintance."

Dolly blushed becomingly. "Would you please come in? All of you. Our home is yours and I can't wait to hear about your trip." She was graciousness personified and when Adam winged out his arm to her, she smiled demurely and accepted.

Emily looked at her sisters, who nodded in

approval. Cyrus offered Liza his arm and Emily linked arms with Junie. "I can't wait to hear about everything. The good, the bad, and the happily ever after."

"It's a long story," Junie warned.

"Full of heartache and danger," Liza agreed. "But in the end, we're family."

Emily met Cyrus's gaze over Liza's head. He winked at her and everything was completely, totally right in Emily's world. "And no matter what, we always will be."

About the Author

Thanks so much for reading this *Jeweled Ladies* story! Leaving an honest review or telling a friend what you thought is the best way to show the love for your friendly local author!

Who is Maggie Chase? Writer, reader, crafter—I've told a lot of different stories a lot of different ways as Sarah M. Anderson, but the Jeweled Ladies series marks my first foray into historical erotica. I passionately believe that every single person deserves their own happily-ever-after and my stories reflect that hope on the page.

Readers can find out more about Maggie any of the following ways:

Sign up for her newsletter:
http://bit.ly/maggiechasenews

Visit her website:
http://www.maggiechase.com

Check out her Tumblr:
http://themaggiechase.tumblr.com/

Follow on Twitter:
http://twitter.com/TheMaggieChase

Leave a review on Goodreads:
http://www.goodreads.com/maggie_chase

Get Amazon pre-order information:
www.amazon.com/author/maggiechase

Other Books by Maggie Chase

The Jeweled Ladies: The Mistress Series

His Topaz
Their Emerald
Her Ebony
His Sapphire
His Crown Jewel

The Jeweled Ladies: The Rogues Series

His Diamond
His Amethyst

Now Available from Maggie Chase

One night will solve her problems—if she can go through with it.

Cam Douglas wants to go straight but he needs cash, so he takes one last job—robbing the bank in Brimstone. He visits the Jeweled Ladies for an alibi but somehow winds up buying a virgin at an auction. He has no intention of forcing the girl, but when Miss Diamond insists on being deflowered, he's too much of a gentleman to say no to a lady.

Read on for an excerpt of
HIS DIAMOND
A Jeweled Ladies story

Cam scratched at his neck. He'd prefer not to hang over this job, but what the hell. Someone wanted the First Macon County Bank robbed. They had a plan—a damned good plan, Cam knew. Better than anything he could come up with. They just needed the hired muscle to actually pull off the job.

"I don't know," he said, mostly to himself. "Seems risky."

Hatfield spat again, but this time in agreement.

"I mean, if I want to rob a bank, I'll rob a bank," Cam went on, pivoting on his heels and walking away. "I'll do it for myself. For us," he added, mindful that he was not the boss of Hatfield. They were a team. "Not for some shadowy figure that doesn't want his hands dirty."

Hatfield grunted, which was practically the same thing as him shouting in agreement.

"Then you gotta ask yourself *why*," Cam went on. "Why does this man want to rob this bank on that specific date, in that specific way? Yeah, there's the money, but it feels like a setup," he concluded, looking back at the bank.

Hatfield made a sound of warning, but by then it was too late—Cam had collided with someone. "Oof!"

The first thing he thought was *soft*, followed quickly, and strangely, by *purple*.

Mine was the third thing.

He moved without thinking, wrapping his arms around the girl's waist to keep her from falling onto her backside in the middle of the dirty street. He hauled her against him and spun, struggling to keep his balance so he didn't topple them both. That feat of acrobatics brought her breasts in full contact with his chest. He stumbled as something in his brain misfired, repeating *Mine*. He clutched her even tighter and in that moment, there was no hope of finding his balance. He staggered backward, tripping and going down like a sack of bricks, the back of his head bouncing off the boardwalk. The woman landed on top of him with a gasped, "*Oh!*"

His head ached dully, but she was sprawled on top of him, his arms around her waist, her weight pressing down against him. She felt so good there and his body leapt to appreciate her properly.

Yeah, he didn't give a damn about his head.

He got his eyes to focus at the same moment she pushed herself up, her hands flat on his chest. Which drove her hips against his. God, she was going to kill him and he was going to die a happy man.

Then the full impact of her appearance hit him, harder than any boardwalk ever could. Her hat had been knocked aside, revealing a riot of gorgeous blonde curls. His hands had already started tracing a path up her back toward that hair before he got them under control.

But that wasn't the worst part. No, the worst part was her eyes, a pretty light blue that was like the summer sky on a perfect day. She was the most stunning woman he'd ever fallen for.

"Beautiful."

"I beg your pardon?"

Shit, had he said that out loud? He must have hit his head harder than he'd thought. "Apologies, Miss," he said quickly because it was the only thing he could come up with.

She pushed against his chest again and damned if he didn't want to pull her right back down into his arms.

A look of alarm crossed her face. Oh, right. They were lying in the middle of the boardwalk. She was on top of him. People were probably beginning to stare. He sat up, which led to her straddling his lap, her skirts tangling around both their legs.

"My apologies," he said again, forcing himself to let go of her. "I didn't see you there."

215

Hatfield appeared, grabbing the elbow of the young lady and hoisting her to her feet.

"The fault was mine," the blonde said, adjusting her hat and trying to get her curls tucked up under the brim again. "I was distracted."

Now that she was no longer on top of him, Cam got a good look at her and his mouth fell open. The girl wore a gown of lustrous purple silk so dark it was almost black, cut to show off the sweeping expanse of her bosom without being vulgar. Her hair was swept up, generous curls rioting out from under the brim of her broad hat.

This girl was the loveliest woman he had ever seen and he had seen a lot of lovely women. She was sweet and young and innocent-looking, like she didn't have a care in the world. At the sight of her, something sighed in his chest. True beauty was so rare in his world. He appreciated it all the more when he did see it.

Mine.

He had no claim to this girl, no right to even look at her, much less hold her in his arms. But tell that to his body.

Don't miss
HIS DIAMOND
By Maggie Chase
© 2017 by Maggie Chase
Sign up for the Newsletter
Check out www.maggiechase.com
for more great Jeweled Ladies stories!